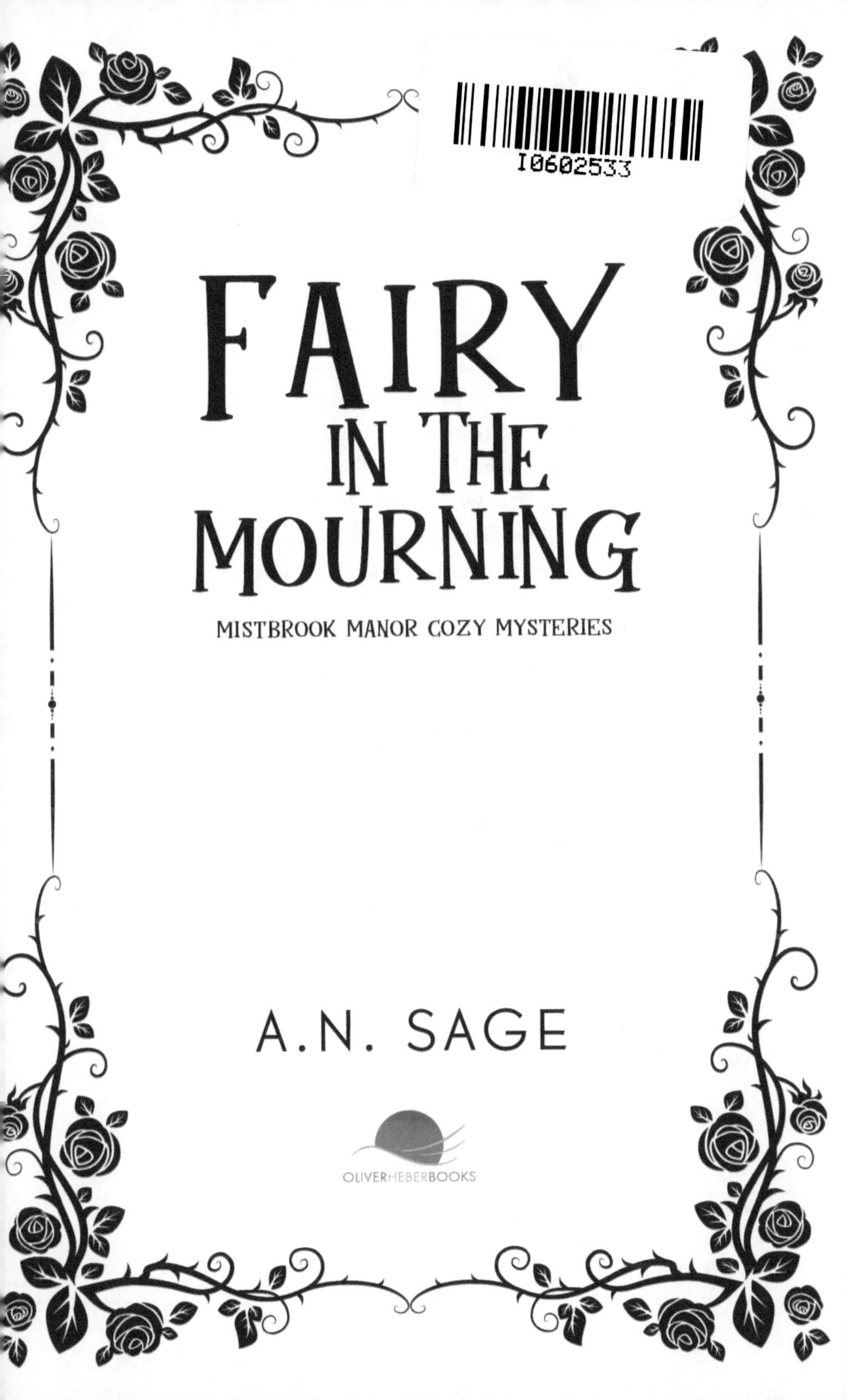

FAIRY
IN THE
MOURNING

MISTBROOK MANOR COZY MYSTERIES

A.N. SAGE

OLIVERHEBERBOOKS

Contents

Chapter One

It was decidedly strange how quickly I became accustomed to dead bodies. All par for the course since I was a funeral director in our quaint little town of Orchard Hollow, but still strange, nonetheless.

Sure, I was always a recluse, even before I shot myself through the portal from Fairy to the human realm. Back home, I tended to spend most of my time with the flowers in my mother's royal garden, much to the dismay of my father. And yet, no matter how the king insisted I socialize, I pulled away. I did not need the anxiety of trying to make friends. Being a fairy with a secret ability to open portals was bad enough. No way would I add social horror on top of it.

That was likely why I escaped with nothing but my

wings on my back and not so much as a goodbye at the first mention of an arranged marriage.

But I digress. What was I thinking about again? Oh, yes. The dead ones.

I glared at the open casket before me, my head tilting and my eyes tracking the glimmer of the sunlight reflecting on the ivory silk interior of the box. The model was a fine one. A deep mahogany, polished to a mirror finish in a warm, reddish hue. There were intricate carvings of roses and ivy from solid gold, shaped like curling vines that twined toward the center, where a small inlay of mother-of-pearl depicted a bird in flight. The roses were a nice touch and my favorite part of the piece, though I was partial to flowers being a green fairy and all. The hinges of the casket were hidden from view and made no sound when I closed the lid, revealing more of the carvings etched throughout.

It truly was breathtaking, even for a casket.

Which was exactly why I had it specifically brought in for the man in the display room with me. This one, however, was not dead at all.

I peeled my gaze from the casket to look at Henry Barlow. His beard was perfectly trimmed today, as it had been nearly each time he visited me this past year. Henry had become quite the regular at the funeral home. It wasn't unusual for people to make visits when planning out their final days; in fact, some stopped by several times to finalize details. Henry, though, was a whole other story. The man practically lived here.

I knew the Victorian manor I ran the funeral home out of had no shortage of rooms, my own living quarters included, but the amount of times Henry came by was bordering on the obsessive.

Today was no exception.

"Well, what do we think?" I asked the town historian. "It's a beauty, isn't it?"

Henry ran a bony hand through his salt and pepper hair, then trailed his fingers along the wood top of the casket. "Sure is," he said softly. "You really have an eye for these things, Lyra."

"It comes with the territory," I replied with a smile. "Kind of like you and knowing details that no one else would guess at."

"Ha! Touché. I suppose researching for a living comes with its benefits," Henry said. He raised his pointer finger and pointed to the black-and-white photograph of the Orchard Hollow cemetery hanging in the gilded frame on the wall. "Speaking of which, did you know that the cemetery wasn't always a place to bury our dead?"

I shook my head. Frankly, I didn't know much about the history of the town I accidentally ended up in. When the portal spewed my sorry behind into this realm, the first place I visited was the cemetery. It was where I met the previous funeral director and the spot that solidified my future here. Other than the location of specific graves that belonged to people passing through the Mistbrook Manor Funeral Home, I knew little about the place.

I really should have asked Darius for a history lesson before he handed over the keys to the manor and left me in charge. We had plenty of time while I was getting certified to run the place, but it never came up. I was simply happy to have a home again.

Eyes narrowing, I shook off the wayward memories that seemed so long ago now and faced Henry. "What was it before then?" I asked.

A twinkle lit up Henry's blue-gray eyes.

Oh my. Here we go.

"Well," the historian started. "Back during the Civil War, the area was used to safeguard all the town's most needed possessions. Weapons, gold, they even had a building dedicated to the storage of rationed foods. Essentially, anything that could be used to aid the people living here while the war raged on."

I blinked rapidly, amazed by the new information. "Really? Why did they turn it into a cemetery?"

"It's quite an interesting story, actually. Because of the so-called treasures held there, the place was highly targeted by the opposing army. Many died defending their possessions and since times were bleak and resources were scarce, they left the bodies there."

"Right next to the food?"

Henry nodded. "Sometimes, yes. After a while, there were more bodies than goods, so someone had the bright idea to make the place into a cemetery instead. It's been that way ever since." He glanced at the photo, inspecting the open iron gate and the decorative carvings along it. "Fascinating, no?"

"It's something, all right."

I kept a rigid smile as I forced the images of corpses on top of apples out of my head. I should have known better than to ask Henry to expand. The man had been coming here for almost a full year to plan his own funeral meticulously should he happen to leave us ahead of the natural schedule and he always had a morbid story to tell. I knew that Henry was a stickler for details. It made sense considering what he did for a living in the college a few towns over, but today's tale took the cake. I desperately wished to wash it out of my brain.

"That reminds me, did you know that they used to use old lemons to send secret messages to the soldiers during the war?" Henry asked. "Lemons were great for writing hidden messages. A little heat and poof! Message revealed."

I scratched my head, unsure how we got here.

As if on cue, a soft fluffy gray tail rubbed against my leg. I looked down to find Theo walking figure eights between my feet, his expression expectant.

"I see I have held you up from the man of the house long enough," Henry said.

I chuckled, nudging the toe of my shoe under Theo's back paw. "He wishes," I joked. "But I should get going. Where did we land on the coffin?"

"I'll take it!" Henry exclaimed. "Add it to the final plans and send me the revised budget. I'd like to get things finalized as soon as possible."

An awful dread filled my stomach with acid. My gaze rested on the historian, darkening. "Is everything okay, Henry?"

For a moment, he didn't speak, and shivers broke out on my skin. Was Mr. Barlow sick? Could the reason for his frequent visitations have been more than a man wishing to be prepared for the inevitable? I frowned. How could I have missed it? I was usually quite adept at reading people; it was how I managed to stay away from most of them.

The historian sighed. My heart dropped into my shoes.

"Everything is fine, Lyra," he said. "I have some things in the works that will be ... eventful. I was hoping to check tasks off my list so I could focus on them, that's all. All our time is numbered, a mirror of what we have left on this plane, after all."

I let go of the breath I held with a whoosh. *Whatever that means.* At my feet, the cat scratched at the floor, a sure sign that he was in need of his afternoon snack. Or else.

Picking up my laptop, I pulled up Henry's account and added the mahogany coffin to the growing list of items. The total sum glared back at me from the screen, and I swallowed hard, realizing that Henry was spending a small fortune on his farewell. Somehow, it was nice to see someone care this deeply about their funeral. It told me that Henry knew his life mattered, and he wanted to celebrate it when he was gone. I looked around at the coffin displays surrounding me. Some things were just worth the money.

I wished Henry a good day and walked him to the front door. As I watched him start up his Mini Cooper and drive down the driveway, my mind kept returning to the cemetery story. *Thanks, Henry,* I thought, my gaze trailing the gravel the car kicked up. *Now I'll never sleep again.*

I looked across the front yard of the manor, past the rose bushes and toward the drop-off of the cliffs leading down to the sea. The waves clashed in the distance, bringing with them the sound that always relaxed my bones. I slumped my shoulders, leaning against the open doorway. Before me, the sprawling porch crawled with shadows as the sun made its rotation in the sky. It was a gorgeous day, the promise of spring nearly in the air.

"He is right, you know. I *am* the man of this house."

The muscle in my jaw twitched. I rolled my shoulders, my spine growing rigidly straight as I turned my gaze downward. Below me, stretched across the threshold, was Theo. His whiskers twitched as he opened his mouth to speak again, then thought better of it.

Oh, did I forget to mention? Theo is a changeling. One who was frustratingly stuck in a cat's body because of his terrible attitude and a fight with someone over in assignments on Fairy's side of things. If it wasn't for his talent of not being able to keep his mouth shut, I may have been free of the bratty creature.

No such luck. Unfortunately.

I gave him a nudge with my foot. "You are barely the pet of the house, Theo."

"It's Theodore," the cat corrected. "How many times must I ask you to use my full name? Are the added syllables too much to handle?"

A headache careened between my temples from having to argue with the changeling again. Despite Theo being my only company in a very large, very empty manor, the ping-pong insults were a lot to handle on days when all I wanted was some quiet time. Maybe curl up with a book and a steaming cup of tea. Or stare at the peeling floral wallpaper in my bedroom for hours. Anything but this.

I rolled my eyes skyward. "I should do some gardening while the sun is out," I said, hoping he got the point.

"What you should do is go check on that portal again," Theo suggested. "Ever since your lover-boy returned, I've been walking on eggshells."

I crooked a brow at the cat. "Why are you so worried? If the Prince of the Shadow Court is in this realm, it isn't you he's after." My stomach churned and my knees knocked as I thought about the horrible man that slipped through my portal. I forced myself to think clearly, the vise on my heart loosening slightly. "Besides, we don't know for certain it was Rhyven who killed the roses. Last I checked, the portal was still secured."

"Please," Theo drawled. "We both know it was him. Killing your monstrous flowers was a warning."

The lump in my throat heated up. "A warning of what?"

"I don't know. But you left the man high and dry when you skipped out on your engagement, so I'd sleep with one eye open if I were you."

I didn't have the heart to tell him that I had been doing that since the moment I left Fairy. Theo was dramatic and often over the top, but he wasn't wrong. I fled a commitment my father made to a powerful court

—a hand in marriage was a binding contract, one that few broke and lived to talk about. Add that to my ability to open portals and being the first fairy to do so in centuries made me a hot commodity on that side of the portal.

Life was nothing if not eventful.

"Speaking of the roses," I said, attempting to change the subject. "I should go see how they're holding up. It took almost all my magic to bring them back to life and they are still not fully recovered."

Theo's paws stretched out in front of him, the gray fur cascading over the wooden planks of the floor. "Here's an idea. Why not chop them all down instead? Make a day of it."

"Why do you hate my joy?"

"Because it usually smells like manure."

Ignoring his snide remarks, I left the cat in the front hall, put on a warm sweater, and made my way to the rear of the house. As I walked, my feet padded softly on the floor, the house absorbing the hushed sound and replacing it with its own groans. The smell of wood varnish filled my nostrils, and I inhaled it deeply, my nerves instantly calming. As I passed the grand staircase leading to the second floor, my movement caused the chandelier to twirl and lights glimmered all around me, reflecting off the soft varnish of the decorative wood panels lining the walls.

Mistbrook Manor was probably the coziest place I had ever stepped foot in.

I reached the door leading to the basement morgue and gave the handle a twist to confirm it was closed. I had locked it earlier, but one could never be too careful when it came to caring for the dead. Security was of the utmost importance. Especially for me.

When I stepped closer to the back door, I started for my gardening tools hanging on the hooks near the exit but stopped. My back straightened as I reached into my jeans pocket to grab my vibrating cellphone. My eyes narrowed on the flashing screen.

"What now?" I whispered.

It appeared the roses would have to wait for the time being. I wiped my brow and pressed to accept the call. Another one of my secrets came knocking.

Chapter Two

Towering bookcases surrounded me as I pushed open the bronze door buried beneath the Starling Family Mausoleum and stepped inside. The smell of old tomes and burning wax pierced my nostrils, and I inhaled it greedily, glad to be back in the secret hiding space that lay deep underground. When I first stumbled upon it after following Finn O'Malley, the hospital morgue director who posed as a detective and broke into my home, I nearly fainted from the sight. No one in town knew about this place, which was what made it the best meeting spot for Grim Wardens.

And there you had it—my dirty little secret.

I looked around the hidden library, my eyes landing on the three people sitting at the circular oak table in the center. The low light of the space made them appear ominous, with dark shadows under their eyes, but I knew them as anything but. For a group of undertakers in a secret society devoted to solving crimes, they were a surprisingly lovely bunch.

"Lyra! You made it!" Mortimer, the oldest member of the group, exclaimed.

He straightened out his tie and brushed away invisible dirt from his staple five-piece suit as he rose to greet me. His nearly white hair showed like a beacon under the overhead light, and I noticed that he took extra care of it today. I wondered if his recent rendezvous with a certain librarian had something to do with it.

I smiled, hanging up my tweed coat on the rack near the door, and walked deeper into the library. The place was built by an eccentric relative of Finn's late wife and was an exceptional nod to the past. From the intricate design of the vaulted ceiling—made to sustain the weight of all that cemetery earth above us, I bet—to the candelabras lining the walls, it was a true masterpiece of architecture. It was no big shock the group chose it for their meeting place. The hidden library lent itself to the work they did: solving crimes the police didn't want to touch.

I supposed that included me now too, since I agreed to join them.

Fixing my unruly curly hair, I waved, saying, "Hi, everyone. Want to fill me in on what happened?"

"What didn't happen?" Ellie said. The youngest group member was scowling, as usual, and had her round thin-framed glasses so low on her nose they teetered on falling off. She finally noticed and shoved them back into place before saying, "Finn had a run-in with the police at the hospital last night."

My gaze rolled past Ellie to Finn beside her. His tousled hair fell in loose waves over his forehead and when he raked rough fingers through it, the muscles in his arms bulged. My skin heated, and I had to remind myself that we were surrounded by other people, and I was much too old to be having a schoolgirl crush on a coworker. Even if that coworker did ask me out on a date not too long ago.

A date we were yet to go on.

I frowned, then realizing no one was privy to my inner turmoil, fixed my face and lowered to sit at one of the empty chairs around the table.

"The police?" I asked Finn, avoiding his brown eyes entirely. "That can't be good."

The morgue director smiled with all his teeth, his head shaking. "Not in the least. They had some questions about a case we helped with last year, a string of robberies that ended in an unfortunate casualty."

"Did they catch whoever did it?" I asked.

Finn nodded. "They sure did. But the trial is coming up, and they wanted me to go on record," he replied. "To corroborate their story."

My brow furrowed. I rolled my gaze around the table. Surely, I was missing something because I didn't understand why this would be such an issue for the Wardens. After all, they made it clear that the entire purpose of the society was to help the police bring down criminals. Why would this be any different?

I was about to ask when Ellie said, "He can't go on the stand without telling everyone about the society."

Oh. That is an issue.

"Is there any way to get out of this?" I asked. My head swung around again, suddenly realizing we were short a member. "Where is Rosemary?"

The fourth member of the group and Ellie's business partner at the funeral home they ran was never absent. In the few months I spent with the Wardens, I could always count on Rosemary to be on time, if not early, for the society's impromptu meetings. And one as important as this would not be something she'd brush off.

I folded my arms over my chest, questions filling my mind to the brim.

"She's taking the day off," Ellie said. "Her mom is in town and it's ... a mission."

Flashes of my own mother raced through my head, and I had to tamp them down before I broke down into tears. How long has it been since I saw her? I stopped counting the years at this point because it only made me all the more upset. If it wasn't for that horrible marriage arrangement, I wouldn't have had to leave her behind. My father and I were never on the greatest terms, but mom was special. Our relationship was special. On some days, I missed her so fiercely it physically hurt to breathe.

I blinked away the hot tears gathering behind my lids and focused on Ellie. "I hope she isn't too stressed out."

"Any visit from Her Royal Highness, Mrs. Singh, is bound to be stressful," Ellie said. She tightened the straps on her oversized denim overalls. "But it's nothing Rosemary isn't used to by now."

"Rosemary is a princess?"

The mortician dropped the straps and looked at me quizzically. "I mean that ironically."

My cheeks flushed, and I cleared my throat. What was going on with me today? Obviously, Rosemary wasn't a princess. Not everyone belonged to a royal family in this realm.

I mentally slapped myself. *This isn't Fairy.*

The mere thought of my home made my skin break out in goosebumps. My spine straightened as nerves raked their talons down my back and legs. I shivered. *Concentrate on the now,* I told myself. *It has been months since the roses were destroyed and no appearance from Rhyven. You are safe.*

I counted back from ten, breathing through each number. No matter how I spun it, I didn't feel all that safe anymore, and it was beginning to show.

The cracks in my carefully orchestrated life were widening.

"All that aside," I said to the group. "How can I help get you out of this situation, Finn?"

The morgue director nudged his chin toward Mortimer. "Morty had an idea that if we find a way to position me as an unreliable witness, the police might revoke their invitation."

"That sounds great!" I exclaimed. "How do we do that?"

"That is the true conundrum," Mortimer said.

I narrowed my eyes at the old man, my lips tightening into a thin line. "You have no idea, do you?"

"Not a clue."

Chuckling, I reached for the small pile of books on the table, noting the spines. It appeared the Wardens started in the most logical place by researching for loopholes in the legal system. I assumed since the police approached Finn in the hospital, the victim of the robbery ended up on a slab in his morgue. It was clever to look for a way out within the legal laws, considering Finn's position as the morgue director in that same hospital. Perhaps he was too close a contact to have an impartial opinion, especially since he helped solve the case.

But was it enough?

I somehow doubted it. I looked at the strained expressions of the people before me. No wonder they were worried. They had every reason to be. If the society was to come to light, people would come knocking on their doors to get cases solved. Not to mention that more often than not, the society operated in secret to avoid stepping on the police's toes, sometimes going as far as to deliver anonymous tips to help solve cases. While our town's sheriff was open-minded to our involvement, not every officer would be on board with a bunch of civilians trying to do their jobs. We didn't represent the cops, and our interference could surely be seen as a problem in a lot of cases.

An idea sparked to life as I trailed a finger over the gilded letters on a book's spine. "Finn, when you were working on this case, did you speak to the robbers firsthand?"

Finn nodded slowly. "Of course. It was how we figured out they were guilty. One of them let a piece of information slip."

"Amateur hour," Ellie added with a smirk.

Mortimer brushed her off, a frown on his face. "Why do you ask, Lyra?"

"I was thinking that if you're trying to disqualify Finn as an expert witness, showing that he might be connected to the opposing side, might do the trick. Maybe." I scratched my head, then turned to Finn. "Didn't you say your brother-in-law is a cop? Could you ask him?"

"That's a great idea!" Finn exclaimed. "And I believe he might be on shift today, so I could stop by and ask him." His eyes landed on me, and he asked, "Want to join me?"

My heart thundered in my chest. A bead of sweat rolled down my neck and the coldness of it bit at my skin like Theo's sharp nails. Was it hot in here? I flushed, my skin suddenly gaining the temperature of the sun's core.

Forcing a meek smile, I said, "Sure. That sounds great. I need to go into town to pick up a few supplies anyhow."

"Perfect," Finn said, rising to stand. "We can stop by the Whistling Kettle for a cup of tea on the way."

Avoiding the smirks from Mortimer and Ellie, I pushed aside the books and stood up. As I trailed behind Finn toward the staircase leading out of the library and back to the world above, all I could think of was what a terrible idea this was. Getting close to Finn was not a solid plan. Especially not now with the possible threat of my very powerful, very angry ex-fiancé looming over me. But how could I say no?

Finn opened the door, his hand pressing to my lower back as I skirted past him to step out. Every bone in my body turned to liquid in response. My head spun and my mouth was as dry as a desert.

Oh, boy. I was in trouble, all right.

I hurried my steps to run up the winding staircase and into the main mausoleum. Dust swirled around me, and I could hear the distant cry of crows outside, somewhere in the heart of the cemetery. I bit down on the inside of my cheek. Perhaps the chill in the air and being surrounded by the dead would help me get my head on straight.

I glanced at Finn's solid build beside me. Somehow, I doubted even that would do the trick. It was time to admit it. I had a huge crush on Finn O'Malley, and it couldn't have happened at a worse time. Wonderful.

Chapter Three

Cliff Row was alive with the hum of the upcoming spring. Sunlight filtered through the branches of the trees that lined the sidewalk and shadows played across the stones as we marched down the street. Around us, shopkeepers propped open their doors with chairs and buckets and bricks. Anything to let in the breeze that had finally started to warm up. The smell of freshly baked bread wafted into my nostrils as we passed the bakery. My stomach growled and for the first time in a very long time, I was grateful for the sounds of chatter around me since it served well in masking the wild animal living in my gut. I rubbed my hungry belly, hurrying to catch up with Finn, who walked briskly down the street.

To my right, a colorful awning flapped against the

wall, and I turned to inspect the window display, a smile broadening on my face. Even the local handmade shop was done with the winter—the soaps lined up in the window were shaped like flowers in every color of the rainbow.

I made a note to pick some up for the manor and rushed further ahead. Catching up with Finn, I glanced at his confident stride, my shoulders instantly rolling straighter to match his. Though Finn wasn't from Orchard Hollow, he maneuvered across the crowded street as though he had been here a million times. Which, I supposed, was highly likely with his wife's relatives being long-time residents. Well, relatives were a stretch. From what I recalled, the Starlings were mostly long gone or relocated elsewhere. Thus, the location of the secret society's meeting place being in the hidden room under the family's mausoleum.

I pressed my lips tightly together. It was a great convenience that someone in that lineage was eccentric enough to require a secret library.

We passed the local coffee shop, Bean Me Up, and I skirted around a family of three sitting at one of the round tables outside. The little girl tugged on her mom's sleeve lightly, pointing to the bookshop sign down the block. By the look on the mom's face this wasn't the first place the kid dragged them to but she nodded and whispered something in the girl's ear which seemed to keep her from running off for the time being. The town was overflowing with new faces today, this family included.

I looked around me, then jabbed Finn in the side with my elbow. "Tourist season started early this year."

"It isn't always like this?"

I shook my head. "Not until summer. And the holidays tend to get fairly hectic," I replied. "But we'd better hurry along. We'll likely be waiting a while for a table, if this crowd is any indication."

As we rounded the corner and saw the people standing outside the Whistling Kettle, my pulse sped up. The line went as far back as the full block, with everyone eager to get inside. There was a couple at the end that couldn't keep their hands off each other and repeatedly elbowed the women in front of them as their displays of affection went from demure to extreme. The women turned to look over their shoulders, shaking their heads at the young man with the rugged face and the bubbly girl hanging off him. At this rate, we'd be lucky to get a table at all. I glanced between the teashop and the pharmacy.

"Maybe we can put our names down and I can pick up the supplies I need for the morgue while we wait."

"Great idea!" Finn agreed, rushing off toward the teashop instantly.

While I waited for him to return, I took out my phone and read over the list of supplies I'd jotted down that morning. The pharmacy in town should have most of the items—Jennifer kept the place well-stocked for the most part. I wondered if being a werewolf had something to do with her immaculate attention to people's needs. Werewolves were notorious for catering to others, a trait that was often overlooked in mythology. Unlike vampires and warlocks, they were actually a very docile bunch.

I checked the list again, settling on only getting the items I urgently needed. We had parked farther away, and I didn't want to make Finn haul my bags with me all through town.

"Looks like a half hour wait," Finn said, sidling up beside me. "Mrs. Dawson said she'll message me as soon as something opens up."

I chuckled, remembering our last interaction with the shop owner. "Any fresh gossip?"

"She was too busy to chat," Finn said. "But if you were curious, Debbie Mantel is pregnant, and Mrs. Dawson is not convinced her husband had any hand in it."

A laugh bubbled out of me. I slapped Finn's arm, gripping it as I continued to cackle like a deranged bird. Tears filled my eyes, and I swiped them away, finally calming down.

I looked up at Finn. "I really *did* need to know that information."

"Gripping stuff," he teased.

Still giggling, I put my phone back in my pocket and turned toward the pharmacy. As I did, I completely misjudged how many people were on the street and my head smashed into someone's chest with a loud thud. Stars swarmed my vision, my brain rattling from the sudden impact. I blinked rapidly and rubbed my forehead as I battled the blurriness in my eyes away.

When I finally gained some focus, my mouth gaped in surprise. I looked at the tall man I nearly ran over. "Henry? Hi! What brings into town?"

Henry Barlow's face lost color fast. He glanced over his shoulder, his fingers twitching at his sides as if he was itching to grasp for something to hold. He jerked his arms up and into the pockets of his light brown tweed coat. A sheen of sweat glistened on his brow, and he was completely unaware when it rolled down into his eyes, blinking it away with little care.

"Oh. Hi, Lyra," he said. His words came out clipped and almost well-rehearsed. "I have a few things to pick up before the big event this weekend."

I crooked a brow at him. "What event?" Then, noticing his continued discomfort, added, "Is everything all right?"

Henry waved me off.

"Excuse me. I am a tad scattered with all the preparation. I am hosting a presentation in the library on

Saturday, and it is quite a doozy." He looked between me and Finn. "You two should come!"

"What's it about?" I asked at the same time as Finn said, "Sounds great."

Henry chuckled, but it came out strained and cough-like. His hands seemed unable to stay still, and he fiddled with his fingernails to keep them busy. His eyes narrowed on an empty spot on the street beside us, then darted back to Finn and me. "I have been working on this presentation for years. I suppose you could say it is my life's work," Henry explained. "Have you two heard of the Hollow's Hoard?"

Both of us shook our heads negatively.

"Well, all the more reason to stop by!" His gaze shot to a middle-aged woman not far from us. "Now I do have to run, I'm afraid. But do me a favor and search for the Hollow's Hoard online. I promise it will intrigue you enough to come. And I will send you the details later today."

He extended his hand, and I took it without hesitation, shaking it lightly. After Finn did the same, Henry bid us a second goodbye and rushed off down the street toward the woman. His steps grew quicker and more mechanical as he approached her. I kept watching them, my fascination with the odd interaction unrelenting.

The knot in my stomach insisting that something

wasn't right with Henry probably had a lot to do with it, too.

As Henry neared the woman, her lips turned down into a sneer. She reached for the bag sitting on the ground next to her, shoving it into Henry's chest with enough force to make him teeter backward. Though the historian wasn't facing me directly, I could see his jowls tense even from where I stood.

I nudged Finn, my chin jutting out toward the scene at the end of the street. "What do you think that's about?"

"I don't know," Finn said. "But it looks serious."

I peeled my attention away from him. Now Henry and the woman had their arms up, each one flapping angrily as they exchanged heated words. It was impossible to make out the words from here, but it was obvious they were in the middle of an argument. And a bad one at that.

A second later, Henry put his palm out to stop the woman from speaking further. He reached into the bag and pulled out a plastic box with wires hanging off of it. I squinted to make out the machine better, realizing it was an old-school slide projector. I saw Henry inspect the projector, then, seemingly satisfied, deposit it back in the bag.

He glared at the woman. She gritted her teeth in return.

"What is going on with him today?" I whispered. "Henry is usually very calm. I've never seen him so worked up before."

Finn shrugged. "He's probably nervous about the presentation."

"Maybe."

I kept one eye on Henry and the woman who continued their shouting match. A few moments later, Finn's phone buzzed in his hand as Mrs. Dawson messaged to announce an open table at the teashop. Reluctantly, I left Henry to his battle and followed Finn back to the shop.

My eyes widened. "Shoot! We didn't have time to get my supplies."

"We can pick them up after," Finn said. "Let's get that table before we lose our spot in line."

Looking at the line outside the shop, my brow creased in confusion. The amount of people waiting to sit down appeared to have doubled since we left, and people were joining as we passed. I wondered what all the commotion was about, but my thoughts were derailed by a few words hanging in the air. I slowed my pace, my ears perking.

"I don't know where he came from, but that man better watch out," a sing-song voice said not far from me. "I didn't see a ring on his finger, and you know how some ladies can be in the town."

"I certainly do," another woman agreed. "An eligible bachelor that looks like that is going to get a *lot* of attention."

They laughed.

"I hear Nancy Steeles already has her eyes on him and he'd only shown up a few days ago."

Another chuckle. "Can you blame her? Tall, dark and handsome has Nancy written all over him."

My stomach muscles tensed, and my spine grew rigid. In my chest, my heart galloped as I slowed down further to overhear the women's conversation better.

It can't be.

"Don't forget the tattoo," the first woman said.

The second woman giggled. "How could I? What was it again?"

"You know, I'm not sure. Some sort of swirls? They were quite odd. Almost as though they moved when you looked at them too long." She cleared her throat. "Not that I spent a lot of time looking. I am a married woman, after all."

They laughed again, but this time, I couldn't hear the rest of what they said. The hum in between my ears was too deafening. I swallowed, the saliva pooling in my mouth, my throat suddenly too full.

Not swirls, I thought. *Shadows.*

There was only one man I knew who had a living tattoo. Rhyven.

My knees knocked as I stood stock still in the middle of the street. Ahead of me, Finn turned to glance over his shoulder, concern lining his features when he saw me. I must have looked like a real mess. Not that it mattered. Not anymore.

I looked around the street, my neck stretching to check past the tourists and locals. No one stood out. At least not anyone that put the fear of Fairy into me.

"Lyra? What's wrong?" Finn asked.

Fear gripped my shoulders, yanking them tight. I looked up at Finn. Inside, regret bloomed like a thorny new bud. "I'm so sorry," I said. "I need to take a rain check today."

"What's going on?"

"Nothing to worry about," I said, already backing away. "A cat emergency back at the manor. I'll text you later."

Before he could ask any more questions—like how a cat could call in an emergency—I turned on my heels and bolted down the street. In my escape, I kept a good watch on every face I passed. Not one matched Rhyven's description, and yet I couldn't help but feel like I was being watched.

Followed even.

Dashing through bodies of passersby, I jumped into the first available taxi and slammed the door shut behind me. As we drove off, I thought I saw Finn running out after me, but there was too much of a crowd to make him out. Tears welled behind my lids. Whatever kind of a relationship I thought I could have with Finn could never happen, not with Rhyven in town.

It had to be him the women were talking about. Which meant only one thing.

I had to disappear again. I had to leave Orchard Hollow as soon as possible. Before I paid with my life and the life of everyone I had grown close to.

Chapter Four

"Is this truly necessary?" Theo asked as he watched me shove random items into a duffel bag.

I shot the cat a death glare, my hands moving fast to locate the next useless thing I had grown attached to. My eyes landed on an antique brass napkin ring. I grabbed it hungrily and laid it atop the pile I'd collected in the last hour I spent packing up my entire life. My gaze scanned the room. Where did I leave my watch? I should probably pack it as well. After a few attempts to locate the piece, I gave up and returned my attention to the cat.

My shoulders slumped in defeat. "Did you not hear what I said? Rhyven is here. In town. It's not conjecture anymore," I stated. "We have to hide."

"I beg to differ."

My movements slowed. I turned a narrowed gaze on the changeling. "You don't think we should be worried?"

"I don't think *I* should be worried," the cat said nonchalantly. "You should definitely hit the road." I rolled my eyes skyward. A part of me knew Theo was being facetious and mocking my overreaction to the Shadow Prince's arrival—he had told me so himself the second I returned home. Yet a bigger part of me was too afraid to find out otherwise. I had seen firsthand what the Shadow Court was capable of, and I had no intention of tying myself to that nightmare of a royal bloodline. No, thank you.

I'd rather live under a rock for the remainder of my life than return to Fairy with Rhyven.

I crammed a pair of gardening shears into my purse, frowning. My gaze rolled over the manor and my stomach sank into my boots. I would miss this place fiercely. Other than Fairy, Orchard Hollow and this funeral home had become another home to me. Not waking up in the mornings with the sunlight streaming in through the slats of the ancient window shutters, not smelling the fresh scent of bleach mixed with wood polish as I walked downstairs, not tending to my roses ... it was going to shatter me. But what choice did I have? I'd have to give up all those things once Rhyven came for me anyhow.

No. Best to leave now and on my own terms.

"How can you even be certain he's here to take you back?" Theo asked.

I quirked a brow his way. "Why else would he come?"

"No offense, but there are plenty of other eligible fae women that he could have his pick of. Fae men too," Theo said. "You think the prince actually traveled to another realm for you when he could simply point a finger and be wed already?"

My hands dropped into my lap; the silk scarf I was holding floating down to the floor. In front of me, Theo's questioning glare burned into me as I considered his words. The cat had a point. Not about the prince's options. That was not what gave me pause. Rhyven was a cruel and terrible fae that would no doubt follow me to the end of eternity to prove a point and exact his revenge. I had no doubt of that. When we were children, I saw him frame another fae kid for treason against the crown all because the boy climbed a tree Rhyven favored. Tracking me to Earth and forcing me to marry him publicly was not something I'd put past him.

But how did he get here?

The chances that the prince had found another portal fairy were slim to none and since I didn't open the doorway, how did he come through?

My body froze as another thought occurred to me.

If Rhyven found a door to this realm, was it still open? Could other fae come through?

I raked my fingers through my blonde waves and focused on Theo's furry face. "We can't leave."

"Finally! She sees reason."

"No, I mean not yet," I corrected. "We need to find the portal he used and close it before more of his friends show up. I can't let those monsters anywhere near Orchard Hollow. It would be a disaster."

The changeling cocked his head, his whiskers twitching. "Isn't the town overrun with paranormals?"

"Paranormals, yes. Fae, no. I think we both know that nothing good can come from our kind coming to Earth."

Theo's undignified expression darkened. "Speak for yourself. Changelings have been living in this realm for generations without causing any trouble for the humans."

"Outside of stealing their children to raise as your own back in Fairy?"

"Those kids are living their best life, and you know it!"

I shook my head, zipping up the duffel. Crouching next to the side table in the hallway, I slid the bag under it. "Whatever you say," I said mockingly. "Now, about the—"

My words got cut off by the sound of an urgent

knock on the front door. The house rattled from the sudden interruption, as though it mirrored the panic that twined around my heart. I glanced at Theo, then darted my eyes to the heavy wood door. The locks I installed when I moved into Mistbrook Manor were all engaged, and I made sure to close the deadbolt when I came in. Those precautions, with the combination of protection runes imbued with my fairy magic carved into the doorway, ensured I was as safe here as anywhere.

And yet the second another knock rattled the door, my heart jumped into my throat.

I pulled myself together and stood up on liquid legs. The floor seemed to float beneath me as I made my way to the front, Theo on my heels. He must have been worried as well, because he would never volunteer to greet a guest.

There was every chance this particular guest was unwanted, of course.

Flashes of Rhyven's hard, angular face flashed before me as I reached a trembling hand toward the first lock. One by one, I undid the latches and twisted the locks open, each flick of the wrist sending shivers of fear down my spine. My mouth was dry, and my tongue swelled with each harsh swallow. Goosebumps covered my arms and legs.

A shadow passed outside the small oval stained-glass

window in the center of the door. I stopped stock still. My hand hovered above the door handle and as I turned it, every nerve in my body screamed for me to run. Forcing my shoulders into a rigid line, I swung the door open and slammed my jaw shut.

My eyes widened.

"Finn," I said, sagging in relief against the doorframe.

The morgue director took in my horrified expression, then took note of Theo's straight pointed tail before asking, "Is it a bad time?"

I rose on my tippy toes to peer past his shoulders. Releasing the breath I was holding, I opened the door wider for Finn to come in.

"Not at all," I said. "I was only cleaning the place up." *Cleaning it* out *is more like it ...*

As I watched Finn stroll into the manor, a pang of dread blossomed in my chest. This might be the last time I spent time with the morgue director, and my entire body rebelled at the idea. No matter how much I tried to ignore it, Finn had become a staple in my thoughts. We had not known each other for long, and the time we did spend together had mostly been on Warden's business, but I wanted to know more about him. I was drawn to Finn in a way I hadn't been to anyone in my life. At least not romantically.

The mere concept of romance made me think of

Rhyven and bile rose up my throat. I swallowed it down and followed Finn to the living room, where he stood awkwardly beside the bookcase that was half empty now since I'd packed my favorite tomes away.

His gaze traveled over the empty spaces and the streaks of dust left behind. "Going somewhere?"

I shook my head.

"Redecorating," I said, the lie tasting bitter on my tongue. "So ... what brings you by?"

Finn's brows knitted together.

"Come on, Finn," I urged. "If something is bothering you, you can say it."

"I like you, Lyra."

His words took me by surprise. As did the upset expression on his face. I folded my arms over my chest and looked at him. "Um, all right. I like you too. But I think I may be a little less upset about it."

Finn chuckled. "That's not it," he said. "I was hoping we could spend some time together today. Without the others, that is. And when you ran off so quickly, I ..."

"You thought I changed my mind," I finished for him.

"Did you?" he asked. "Because it's fine if you don't feel the same way, but I am not great at the whole dating thing. So, you really need to spell it out for me."

The tension in my chest lessened briefly as I studied

Finn's face. He looked so boyish, fidgeting with his hands and rocking back and forth on his heels that I couldn't help but admire him even more. Fae men were many things, but shy was not one of them. It was endearing to see Finn open up. So much so that it made me want to rethink the whole running away situation.

I couldn't, of course. Could I?

"It wasn't anything you did," I told Finn. "There is a lot you don't know about my past, things that I left behind and never wished to revisit."

Finn leaned in closer to me. "Is it about your home? You never talk about it."

"That's because it's better this way," I whispered. "Safer."

"Are you in danger?"

Concern made his voice tremble. I looked past him to the bay window and the bright red roses in the distance. I couldn't let Finn worry, not when I wasn't ready to share the reason for my behavior with him. Closing my eyes, I forced a faltering smile and said, "Not right now, no. But home wasn't the best place for me, which is why I had to leave. Why I came to Orchard Hollow."

"Well, I for one am really glad you ended up in this town," Finn said. "And I really hope that you can find some time to let me take you out on a date. A proper one."

"I will," I said, even though I had no idea when that time would be.

"Great! How about this weekend?" Finn asked.

I looked around, wincing. To my right, Theo perched on the windowsill and his eyes widened in my direction. He nodded his head toward Finn, then wiggled his whiskers—the cat's way of telling me to go for it.

Theo must have lost his mind, because there was no way I was going to accept the invitation. I wasn't even certain I'd be around on the weekend.

"Come with me to Henry Barlow's presentation," Finn said. "We can grab dinner after at the restaurant on the cliffs."

I arched my brow. "The Cliffside Diner? That place is really snobby."

"Takeout it is, then!" Finn exclaimed. His face paled, and he bit his bottom lip. "At least say you'll think about it."

Near us, a cat's meow pierced the awkwardness in the air.

"See," Finn said. "The cat agrees. You should definitely come to the presentation. And Henry was right, the topic does sound too intriguing to miss out on."

My curiosity piqued. I retied the scrunchie holding my hair in place and said, "All right, fine. I will think about it."

"Good. I'm glad," Finn said. "I won't take up more of your time. Spring cleaning can get exhausting." As he strolled past me, he squeezed my shoulder, the touch of his fingers sending lightning bolts down my skin.

"The past haunts all of us," Finn said in a low tone. "I know that better than anyone. All we can really do is live for the future, whatever that may be."

I returned his smile and walked Finn back to the door, my steps heavy and leaden. Was Finn right? Was living for the future the only way forward? But how could I think about the future when my present was in jeopardy?

It was all too difficult to make sense of. I knew that my best bet to get away from the Shadow Prince was to run and not look back. And yet the mere thought of going to the presentation with Finn had me doing mental cartwheels and giggling in joy. Was I willing to risk my life for a date?

I had no clue.

Theo squeezed in between my legs as I opened the door for Finn to leave. The heat from his tiny body calmed my nerves, diffusing some of the fog wrapping around my thoughts. It was only Thursday, which gave me a few days before I had to make a decision and I had to admit, both Finn and Henry had painted a picture of the presentation that was hard to resist. I was almost as excited to see what all the fuss was about as I was about dinner with Finn.

I watched Finn get into his car and drive away after saying goodbye and promising to give him an answer as soon as possible. Perhaps if I was lucky, I would get the date of my dreams before I had to leave town for good.

A farewell dinner. That was a good plan. One last meal and then I hit the road.

My stomach turned.

If the plan was so good, then why did my eyes water when I thought about it?

I shut the door and turned the locks. No point dwelling on it now. I had bags to pack and a business to close down. If only I could use my skills as a funeral home director to bury my past six feet under.

Chapter Five

The Orchard Hollow library was the busiest it had been in its entire existence tonight. I huddled in the corner of the presentation room while Finn slinked off to grab us some drinks before the big event started. To my left, a young couple chatted with the town's librarian and her eyes darted to me every so often, a look of interest sparking behind those thick gold spectacles.

There was no doubt she was wondering what the town's funeral director was doing out and about. After my last encounter with Maggie Halloway, I was sure she painted me as a social pariah since I all but threw her out of the manor. In my defense, I thought she was snooping because of ill intentions. How was I supposed to know that Maggie was writing a book about true crime in the town? Or that she was maybe possibly dating Mortimer?

My gaze drifted to the Warden member in question standing next to Maggie. Even from here I could see there was a clear connection between the two with the way Mortimer hung on Maggie's every word. They were like two teenagers in love, save for the fact that both had not been in their teens for many decades.

Mortimer caught me staring and his skin flushed a bright pink. I averted my gaze. No point embarrassing the man when he was on a date.

Speaking of dates ... What was taking Finn so long?

I craned my neck to see over the crowd that gathered for Henry's presentation, spotting Finn attempting to make his way back with two wine glasses in tow. When he reached me, I noticed a bead of sweat on his forehead that he quickly wiped away.

"That was a mission," Finn said, handing me a glass. "You look great today, by the way. I should have said so earlier."

My skin flushed. I fiddled with my ears to give myself something to do, grimacing when I felt the empty lobes. My favorite earrings went by the wayside as my watch did—collateral damage in my hectic attempt to pack even though I wasn't sure I was leaving yet.

I took a sip, the warmth of the wine relaxing my rattled nerves. "There are a surprising number of people here," I admitted. "Who would have thought that a history presentation would get almost the entire town out and about?"

"Are you kidding? A sunken ship and a possible hidden treasure? I'm surprised the adjoining towns aren't breaking down the doors, too."

A laugh bubbled from my lips. Finn was right. The topic Henry devoted the presentation to—the mysterious Hollow Siren and the treasure that it supposedly carried on board—was very intriguing. It was the reason Theo all but threatened to end my life if I didn't agree to come out tonight. Apparently, the cat was very interested in what happened to the heaps of gold the Hollow Siren carried, though his changeling blood had a lot to do with it. Those guys were gold diggers. Seriously, you could not trust a changeling near anything shiny, especially if it held monetary value. They were basically the magpies of Fairy.

"What do you think the big reveal Henry mentioned might be?" I asked Finn.

He shrugged. "No clue. Think he found the treasure?"

I laughed. "Doubtful," I said. "If I discovered a sunken ship worth millions, the last thing I'd be doing is presenting my finding to a room full of strangers."

"The lady has a point."

We both turned to face the gruff voice interrupting

our conversation. Standing before us at over six feet tall was a man who appeared to have stepped out from a historical novel. Somewhere in his late fifties, the man wore a tweed fedora, and his curly brown hair poked out from the bottom in an unruly mess. He had a well-trimmed beard that had several grays peppering it throughout, and his brown suit reminded me of something Mortimer might wear. Old-fashioned and yet modern all at the same time.

I looked him up and down, my gaze narrowing.

"Oliver Hodge," the man said, extending a hand. "a fellow historian."

Finn gave him a firm handshake, and I followed suit, saying, "Do you have a guess as to what the reveal is?"

"Knowing Henry, it will be something only he is excited about," Oliver replied.

My eyes bugged out. "Are you and Henry friends? He's never mentioned knowing another historian in town."

"We've met on a few occasions."

The blazer Oliver wore flapped open when he moved to readjust his hat. My eyes caught a glimpse of something shiny tacked to the lapel of his vest and I zeroed in on the pin, trying to make out the symbol. It was so small that it was nearly impossible to see, but I noticed a bronze scale set in a triangle. An interesting piece. These historians were always sporting trinkets. I remembered Henry showing off an ancient ring he scoured the internet for, and the thing was so hideous I couldn't understand how anyone would want to wear it. Yet Henry was more than eager to place it back on his pinkie after I had a look.

Go figure.

The lights dimmed, and a microphone was turned on somewhere behind us, the feedback from it making my teeth hurt. I offered Oliver a tight-lipped smile and turned to peer over the crowd toward the makeshift stage at the end of the narrow room. Finn's fingers grazed mine, and he said, "Let's see if we can get closer to the front."

Nodding, I followed him through groups of people knitted tightly together, relieved to leave Oliver behind. Small talk with strangers gave me hives, and the night was already stressful enough with so many people crammed into one small room.

We settled on a fairly empty spot to the right of the stage and set our drinks on the ledge of an empty wall shelf that no doubt had books atop it prior to tonight's event.

"Testing, testing," a familiar voice said from the stage.

I craned my neck to see Henry stand with his shoulders rolled straight back and his lips twisted into a wide smile. The warmth from the man could be felt all the way to where we stood and I could see his excitement clear as day when he set the microphone into a stand and turned on the projector next to him. Henry rocked back and forth on his heels, his eyes surveying the room.

He breathed out slowly, the smile stretching his thin lips. "Welcome everyone. It's wonderful to see so many people here tonight." Henry's eyes landed on me. "And some familiar faces as well."

I raised my drink in salute, waiting for him to go on.

"As you may have guessed, tonight's presentation is an exciting one indeed. At least for history buffs."

"And treasure buffs!" someone shouted from the crowd.

Henry chuckled under his breath, the sound amplified by the microphone making it sound forced, like it had been torn from his throat. "Yes," he agreed. "Those as well. But I am not here for the treasure ... Not entirely. I am here to speak to you about a ship."

He pushed a button on the small remote in his hand and the projector whirred to life with a guttural screech. The white screen behind Henry lit up brightly, an image of a ship docked at port filling it from wall to wall. I looked at the black-and-white photo, my attention jumping over the details hungrily.

"What a beauty," Finn whispered in my ear.

I had to agree. The Hollow Siren was a sight to be seen. It had a wide mast that appeared to stretch for miles, though I knew that was only the angle of the photo playing with my perception of the ship's already massive size. The sails, up and unfurled, took up the majority of the sky as though the ship was trying to block out the sun itself. On the side, the name "Hollow Siren" was painted in decorative script, and an intricately carved depiction of a mermaid took center stage above the hull.

The Hollow Siren was not only stunning, but it took up space. It had the same effect as famous people did when they walked into a room. It took your breath away.

My gaze landed on the dock and the crew of people in the photograph. Their faces were blurry and there were some people just off frame, but there were at least three dozen figures in the picture. A large crew indeed.

My stomach dropped into my boots.

Three dozen people that didn't survive.

"Do you think that was the day it sank?" I asked Finn.

As if he could hear me, Henry pressed a button again, and the screen changed to a new image. This one was not of the ship but of five people, two men and three women. They were definitely from a different era, with lush frilly clothes and hairstyles that would not fit in with today's fashions. The men had long twirly mustaches guarding their upper lips while the women had hair piled so high they added a foot of height to their slender frames. And then there were the bustles of their skirts that jostled for space until it appeared that the clusters of furbelows nearly filled the width of the picture.

"March 16th, 1911," Henry said. "The date Percival Whitmore and his wife, Isadora, boarded the Hollow Siren on an exploratory journey across the Atlantic Ocean."

He pointed to the shorter of the two men and the woman sitting next to him. I briefly raked my eyes over her low-cut gown and the enormous oval pendant hanging just below her collar bone. Though the photograph was lacking in color, I could tell the pendant was gold and, much like everything else on the two figures Henry had singled out, must have cost a fortune.

On stage, Henry's eyes darkened. "The couple was accompanied by Clarence Whitmore, Percival's younger brother, and his wife, Henrietta. As well as her lady's maid, whose name remains unknown," he said. "As you may have guessed, they never returned to Orchard Hollow."

"What happened to the ship?" someone asked.

"That is the subject of much debate," Henry replied. "Some believe it got caught in one of the storms raging in the south and the current carried it off over time, thus it was never recovered. Others think Percival was running from a less than honest business associate and spread rumors of the ship going down to start a new life elsewhere. Others are adamant that something more ... paranormal was at play."

The word made my skin prickle. Was Henry serious? Was there a chance he had magic, and I completely missed it?

I sniffed the air to see if I could detect anything suspicious but came up empty. If there was a paranormal in the crowd, I'd know it.

A few feet from me, Henry laughed heartily. "Of course, it's all hearsay and I can guarantee that no ghosts or magic were involved in the Siren's sinking."

"So, it did sink?" a woman asked.

Henry tsked. "Oh, it most definitely did. And yet no one has ever recovered it. Why?"

He pressed another button, bringing up an image of a current map that was dated to the same month of the ship's departure. "This," Henry said, "is a map of the currents that supposedly dragged our dear Siren to its final resting place. And this—" he clicked again, an image of another map coming into view "—is the map of the journey last shared by Percival with his neighbor. It is the map that helped historians confirm that the ship did, in fact, go down in a storm. Taking its passengers and the trunks of gold and jewels rumored to have been on board with it."

He stalked the length of the stage and back again,

clearing his throat into the microphone. "But what if I told you that I have another theory? One that was never considered before?"

A wolfish grin tugged at the corners of his lips as he pressed the remote to flip the slides. Behind him, the map remained unchanged. Henry tried again with no difference in the result. A muscle feathered in his jaw as he continued to press on the remote, clearly frustrated with his performance derailing.

After several more tries, Henry gave up and stomped to the projector. He opened the plastic top and poked his nose close to the slide deck, his glasses fogging up with breath. A moment later, Henry announced, "Nothing to worry about folks! Just a loose wire." Slowly, he reached in between two slides, his fingers long and steady. "All I need to do is—"

Sparks burst from the projector and illuminated the stage, and Henry, in their bright light. They continued to flash as the projector screeched and hissed, smoke floating up from the slide deck. Hovering above it, Henry's face distorted in pain and his teeth slammed together as the electric current rushed through his body.

"Henry!" I screamed.

The historian did not hear me. His eyes glazed over, and his body vibrated and shook aggressively. Tears flooded my vision as I tore toward the stage with Finn on my heels. There were a few other people that rushed to help, but most stood frozen in shock as Henry continued to be electrocuted.

Heart racing, I climbed onto the stage and slid to a stop a foot away from him. I couldn't touch him, not unless I wanted to get zapped by the current as well.

"What do we do?" I asked Finn in a panic.

"Unplug it!" he shouted.

Our heads twisted right and left to find the cord for the projector. Finn located the wall socket quickly and dove for it, using his scarf to wrap around the cord before yanking it out of the wall. The projector turned off instantly, but there were several brighter sparks as the last of the electricity burned into Henry's skin.

In a flash, the historian's hand pulled free from the slide compartment, and he crumpled to the floor in a motionless heap.

I ran toward him, landing on my knees. Trembling, I reached two fingers toward Henry's neck and felt for a pulse.

"Anything?" Finn asked, standing above me.

My throat closed up. I pulled my fingers away and looked up at him through hot and blurry eyes. My head shook.

Henry Barlow was dead.

Chapter Six

Steam billowed from the mug as Finn slid the tea toward me. I leaned my elbows on the dark mahogany dining table, chest pressed against the delicate filigree carved into the edge. Despite having polished the table only recently, my eyes couldn't help but catch on to every imperfection. The fingerprint marks that dulled the shine in random patches, the small scratch from the time Theo recklessly played with a cat toy on top of it. Even the way the sun glinted on the surface bothered me.

Except that wasn't the real problem, was it? The table was not my main worry.

"I can't believe he's gone," I whispered.

Finn's brows knitted together. "I know. Are you all

right? You and Henry seemed to be close when we ran into him the other day."

"We were friendly. He was a regular at the funeral home," I explained. "I suppose I wouldn't call us friends, but he was a lovely person. A very prepared, super organized person as well."

"I take it he had all the details of his funeral ironed out?"

I shrugged. "Pretty much. At least his family will not need to do any planning, since Henry had his entire service handled. He went as far as to list out the flowers for the wreath."

"I'm sure you helped with that part."

A sad smile tugged at my lips. "I did, yes." I took a sip of the tea and waited for the liquid to warm up my shivering body. The relief never came. "He was here only a few days ago. It's strange to think he will never come around again."

"After Jenny died, I kept looking for her every time I went out. I'd find myself waiting at the cash out line for her to make her way back with added items in tow, or craning my neck over a crowd to see a glimpse of her hair as though we got separated," Finn said. "It takes time to accept loss, even if it's someone you weren't extremely close with. People leave an empty space when they are gone."

My throat swelled as I watched him. Finn's glassy

eyes stared absently out the window behind me, his mouth downturned at the corners. If anyone understood true loss, it was him. It was years since his wife passed away, but the way he spoke of her made my heart break for him. Humans were fickle creatures with souls so breakable I didn't know how they could ever lose one another without shattering.

Now that Henry was gone, I started to understand it a bit better.

I reached over and placed my hand on top of Finn's. "Maybe it's good to remember that space," I said softly. "So, it doesn't feel quite so empty."

The morgue director smiled warmly, and I was instantly aware of his skin touching mine. I pulled my hand back, placing it on my lap. My gaze landed on the grandfather clock next to Finn, and my chest tightened. The day was slipping away quickly. I still had to drop off instructions with the cemetery caretaker for Wednesday's funeral. Mrs. Stokes was adamant about a few details for her father's ceremony, and I didn't want to leave it to the last moment.

I winced, catching Finn's attention. "I can't believe it's already two."

"Really?" he asked, his brows rising high. "I hadn't realized how long we'd been here. I should let you get back to work."

"Are you sure? I don't mean to rush you out."

He brushed me off with a wave of the hand. "It's not a problem. I need to swing by the hospital, and I promised Rosemary to help her move an armoire." He put a finger up to stop me from asking questions. "Trust me, you don't want to know. Let's say Mrs. Singh is particular about furniture placement, and Rosemary wants to keep the peace with her mom while she's visiting."

I grinned. "Well, in that case, I'll leave with you. I need to make a stop as well."

Saying goodbye to Finn was the most awkward experience of my lifetime. Suddenly, I didn't know what to do with my hands and when he reached over to give me a hug, I nearly catapulted backwards. It didn't help that Theo watched us from the windowsill like the little creep he was. When Finn wasn't looking, I stuck my tongue out at the cat and watched his lips move a mile a minute as he cussed me out in true Theo fashion. Luckily, the windows of the manor were soundproofed so Finn didn't hear the troublemaker.

Letting Finn drive off first, I climbed into the truck and gripped the steering wheel. My eyes kept flicking to the house as though I expected to see Henry on the front porch with his briefcase in tow, going on about some historical event like it was the tale of a lifetime.

Finn was right. It would take some time before I made peace with his death.

But what if that wasn't why I was so obsessed with the historian's passing? Something in my gut wouldn't let me put it to rest and, for some reason, I knew it wasn't only because Henry was gone. His death didn't sit right with me.

Shivers tripped down my spine as I recalled the last time I felt this way. I glanced at the clock on the dash. The cemetery caretaker wasn't leaving for the day for another two hours. Plenty of time to make a pit stop first.

I pressed on the gas and peeled out of the driveway, the sense of dread I felt before slightly lessening because of my possibly unhinged plans.

The Orchard Hollow police station was, as always, a depressing sight. The weekend brought in the usual suspects and the torn, worn-out faux leather chairs that lined the left wall in the entrance room were filled with bodies slumped over and reeking of alcohol and sweat. The sounds of mumbles and snoring filled the room, and it made me feel like the walls were closing in on me with every step I took toward the reception desk.

The worn wooden desk lacked shine and luster, and I wondered how long it had been since someone polished the sad thing as I approached. My gaze flicked from the empty chair behind the desk to the heavy door off to the side that was slightly ajar. A security buzzer flashed green next to the handle and there was a draft coming in from the long hallway on the other side of the door. I winced, spotting the locked doors lining the walls. How many people got interrogated in those rooms?

A wide-brimmed hat popped up from behind the desk and I jumped backward, startled. In front of me, Sheriff Romero rose to stand with a bunch of papers and files precariously balanced in his arms. He tossed the pile on the desk with a loud, heavy thud.

The sheriff raised the tip of his hat to wipe his brow, then lowered it back down, concealing his eyebrows. "Miss Moore," he said, glaring at me. "What brings you by?"

I looked around the station, frowning. "Where is everyone?"

"Only me today, I'm afraid," the sheriff admitted. "The patrols are out, and Donna is in Hawaii on vacation." He patted the paper stack grimly. "You know, I never realized exactly how much paperwork this place has."

I laughed. "The cost of small-town businesses is a million paper cuts."

"Exactly." The sheriff's eyes narrowed on me. "So,

what does a funeral home director need at a police station?"

My stomach dropped into my boots as the absurdity of my visit became glaringly obvious. Did I really mean to bother the sheriff—who was obviously drowning in work—with a gut feeling? I bit my bottom lip, ready to apologize and walk away before I made a fool of myself.

An image of Henry's eyes before he died made me stop. I folded my shaking arms over my chest. Whatever doubts I had about how Henry died, I owed it to him to voice them. Even if I was wrong, it was the honorable thing to do.

I sucked in a sharp breath and let it out slowly.

"I wanted to speak to someone about what happened to Henry Barlow," I said.

Romero's face blanched. "The historian? What a terrible thing to have happened. I wasn't at the event, but a few of my officers attended."

"Yes, it truly was awful," I said. "Henry will be missed greatly."

"Were you two friends?"

I shook my head. "We knew each other professionally. But that isn't why I'm here." I cleared my throat. "You're going to think I'm odd, but I was wondering if you were going to be looking into his death."

The sheriff's nose twitched. "Why?"

"I'm honestly not sure," I admitted. "Call it a hunch,

but I think there may be more to what happened to Henry than a faulty wire in a projector."

There was a prolonged, uncomfortable silence as the sheriff stared me down. His thick mustache moved with his lips as he opened and closed them, not speaking. His attention landed on a sleeping man in one of the chairs, then back to me, his expression unreadable.

A moment later, he closed his eyes, rubbing the bridge of his nose, and sighed deeply.

"Do you have any evidence to suggest that the death was anything but accidental?" he asked.

I swallowed hard, saying, "Not exactly."

"Has anyone expressed having ill will toward Henry that you may have overheard?"

My shoulders slumped. "No. Everyone seemed to love him at the event, and he was a very nice person, from what I could tell."

The sheriff grimaced.

"Do you see where I'm going with this?" he asked.

I nodded, defeated. "What you're saying is that my gut feeling is not enough to warrant an investigation."

"What I'm saying, Miss Moore," the sheriff said. "Is that as a law official I have no reason to investigate the accident. As a *law official*, I have to concentrate on active cases that require this department's attention. But *you*, Miss Moore, are free to do as you wish."

Wait, what? Was the sheriff suggesting I investigate this myself?

"In fact, Henry's death was quite strange, as you said," he added. "Strange enough to be a topic of conversation for a certain group of undertakers, I would think."

Oh, he was most definitely suggesting that. I forced a smile, nodding in understanding. "You know about—"

Romero put his hand up to stop me.

"I know nothing," he said, with a twinkle in his brown eyes. "But if you hear anything else that might spur the law's reconsidering of Henry's death, please do give me a call."

Just then, one of the sleepers woke up with a loud groan and the station turned to complete chaos. The man shouted slurred words, all of which were directed at another questionable character a few chairs over. Before I knew it, the two were in a full-on brawl on the police station floor. Arms and legs flailed around, knocking anything not nailed down over.

Romero leaped from behind the table, forgetting our conversation and rushing to break up the rowdy drunks before they hurt themselves. My legs shook as I watched one man attempt to throw a punch at the sheriff and manage to get himself handcuffed to a chair. Romero didn't even break a sweat.

Giving everyone a wide berth, I hurried to the front door, bursting from the station like I was being chased.

As I climbed into the truck and white-knuckled the steering wheel, I couldn't help but glance back at the building behind me. I certainly could have been imagining it, but I was pretty sure the sheriff told me to look into Henry's death.

Perhaps I was onto something after all ... Henry Barlow's death might not have been accidental, which only left me with one theory: someone killed our town's historian and got away with it.

Chapter Seven

I paced the length of the morgue, then back again. To my right, the freezer wall encroached on my personal space and made it harder to breathe. Usually, I enjoyed spending time down in the basement with nothing but silence and the constant hum of the freezers in place of a white noise machine, and yet today my mind would not stop racing. Probably because of the autopsy report in my hands.

Unfolding the now wrinkled piece of paper, I read the findings of the medical examiner over and over again. Not that it provided any new sources of information. According to the report, the cause of death was a very straightforward electrocution. Hard to argue with that.

My brain fogged up. I would have preferred for

Henry's body to be delivered straight here so I could examine it myself, but his next of kin insisted the hospital take over. It would be some time until the body was transferred for funeral arrangements and if it wasn't for Finn pulling strings, I wouldn't even have this report in hand.

Still, I had many doubts and very few answers.

"Why did he appear so agitated lately?" I asked softly.

Behind me, Theo meowed, then said, "The history buff? When was he not agitated?"

"Good point. Henry was always extra excited when he visited. But something seemed off about him during the last few times. Not to mention that he made so many trips here in such a short period."

"What are you getting at?"

I rubbed my temples because I hadn't the slightest clue. "I'm not sure," I said. "It was almost as if he thought my services would be needed soon."

"You think he knew he was going to die?" Theo asked.

"Maybe not. It does sound ridiculous when you say it out loud, doesn't it?"

Theo shrugged, the fur on his back rippling in smooth gray waves. "I have become accustomed to your rather outlandish ideas," he said.

"Yes, well, this one might be too out there, even for

me." A thought popped into my head, and I stopped short. "Unless ... No, that is not possible."

"For the love of Fairy, spill it before I fall asleep."

"You don't think Henry figured out the location of the ship?"

The cat's paw dropped from his mouth mid lick. His amber eyes tracked the swaying of my body in a predatory fashion, and he chittered under his breath before saying, "What ship?"

I smacked my forehead. *Oops.* With everything that happened, I completely forgot to tell Theo about the presentation before it got unfortunately derailed. A sunken treasure was exactly the kind of thing the changeling would get a kick out of.

"Get this," I said excitedly. "Henry's presentation was centered on the Hollow Siren, a ship that mysteriously vanished decades ago."

"So what?" the changeling replied. "Ships sink all the time. It's hardly news to kill over."

I wiggled my eyebrows at him. "It is when there was treasure rumored to have been on board."

The revelation had Theo's full and undivided attention. His paws planted firmly on the desk he perched on, and he leaned in enough to nearly fall off the edge. The cat fixed me with a damning glare. "Treasure, you say?"

"Don't get too excited," I told him. "No one has been

able to find the ship all this time, and not for a lack of trying."

"Your historian may have, though. Now that I know there was a treasure involved, I'd like to change my opinion. I definitely agree that someone may have wanted to kill for the information Henry had. It is an excellent theory that I thoroughly believe you should investigate."

I glowered. "I should have known the promise of gold would have you jumping for joy."

"That and getting you out of the house," Theo said. "Both are wonderful incentives."

I picked up the first thing I got my hands on, a pair of balled up medical gloves, and threw them at the cat's head. The cat darted out of the way expertly and slid off the table, jumping down in perfect form and landing on his paws. His whiskers twitched and his tail hiked up high. "For the sake of finding our treasure, I hope you display better manners," he said, stalking past me toward the stairs. "More bees with honey and all."

I rolled my eyes and turned back to the freezer wall. The doors that lined it stared back at me with cold, metallic glares, each empty compartment a reminder of life that has fled. In the past, when I had doubts about leaving home to come to this realm, I would come down here and sit in silence. Something about the short finality of human life puts things in perspective. Not that the fae lived forever or anything quite so silly. Our lives ended much the same, except for lasting longer.

My eyes widened. At least that was the case for my kind in Fairy. I had no idea how my body would react to living in the human realm. I focused on one cabinet door. Perhaps I would end up in one of those compartments sooner rather than later.

The idea made me shiver, and I peeled my gaze from the doors and turned on my heels, stomping up the stairs to the upper level of the manor. With my thoughts jumbled, there was only one other thing I could try to straighten myself out before I drove myself crazy, thinking of theories for why Henry may have died.

Hastily, I walked to the rear door and grabbed my gardening tools, slipping into a warm sweater and rubber boots on my way out.

When in doubt, garden.

Dirt seeped into my jeans as I sunk down to my knees and got to work. Using the shears, I gently pruned a cluster of dark red roses, carefully removing the spent blossoms. Around me, the smell of the flowers permeated the air and made the tightness in my spine and shoulders dissipate. I sat back to examine the bush before me, looking for any signs of illness or damaged stems. But it was perfect. As always.

I was about to weed the soil when thoughts of Henry popped back into my head. I shook them off, but it was no use—I could not get the historian out of my mind.

"If the treasure wasn't real, why would someone kill you?" I asked the empty garden. "Unless the killer was convinced that it was more than folklore and speculation."

I tried to think of everything Henry mentioned about the Hollow Siren before he died. From what I gathered, he didn't appear to be obsessed with the treasure and much more with the people on board. What were their names? The Whitmores. The couple was a very interesting pair. What was their purpose for the trip? And why go with so few people on board? Surely a ship of that size could carry a larger crew.

Maybe Henry was right. Maybe they were running from the law.

"Two couples and a maid ... No one else."

"What are you rambling about now?"

I spun around to face Theo sitting on a garden bench. "Only wondering why the original couples on the Hollow Siren took the trip in the first place."

"Maybe the wives planned to throw their husbands overboard," Theo said, chuckling. "I hear the ocean is a wonderful way to resolve disputes."

"Theo, will you please—"

I stopped short. My jaw slacked and my lips parted.

Cold air rushed into my lungs as I sat there catching flies and glaring at the cat. A dispute.

"Are you buffering?" Theo asked, his head cocked to one side in question.

I waved him off. "Henry had an argument with someone on the street a few days before the presentation," I said. "A woman. She was the one that gave him the faulty projector! I completely forgot about her."

"The murder weapon."

"Exactly!" I exclaimed. "Do you know what this means?"

The cat yawned, his sharp teeth flashing in the overhead light, then stretched long, his front paws kneading rhythmic circles into the weathered wooden bench. He blinked once—slow, unimpressed—before tucking his paws beneath his chest and closing his eyes. Clearly, I had lost his attention the moment I stopped talking about the ship.

Fine. No matter. I didn't need Theo's approval to solidify the plan already forming in my mind.

I let the shears slip from my fingers, their dull clang against the stone path barely registering as I pushed myself upright. Brushing dirt from my jeans, I exhaled, steadying the restless energy buzzing in my chest.

I had to find the woman Henry argued with. The memory of her face was already hazy, slipping through my brain like water through a sieve. Worse still, I didn't even have a name to anchor her in place.

A flicker of uncertainty stirred in my gut—until realization struck.

There *was* someone who could help. Someone who knew the ins and outs of this town better than anyone. Who could recall birthdays, scandals, and the little details people thought were long forgotten.

And, conveniently, someone who never turned down an invitation for tea and a well-spun tale laced with just the right amount of gossip.

A slow grin tugged at my lips.

If I wanted answers, I knew exactly where to start.

Chapter Eight

The smell of bergamot and vanilla drifted through the air as I sat at a corner table near the entrance of The Whistling Kettle. Near me, three women chatted over freshly poured cups of tea, occasionally pausing their conversation to nibble on the finger sandwiches arranged on the three-tier tower between them. Hovering near the group was Edith Dawson, the owner of the deliciously cozy establishment.

I stifled a laugh as Mrs. Dawson pretended to clear a table that needed no cleaning. Her back arched like a cat's and her ears perked as she leaned in closer to the women to overhear their conversation. She strained, the muscles of her jaw feathering. A moment later, a deflated expression crossed Edith's face. She straightened out, tossing a dishrag over her shoulder and walking to the counter.

It appeared the women were not interesting enough for the town gossip.

There was a cackle of laughter that made me jump, and I noticed Edith's hand shake while she poured hot water from a kettle into a cup. She put the kettle down, running her hand over a wrinkled brow before tucking strands of wayward white hair behind her ears. Today, she wore bright fuchsia earrings that dangled almost all the way down to her shoulders and a flowery top that matched in shade. The colors complemented her olive complexion so well that it made her look like she had just returned from a beach vacation.

Mrs. Dawson spun around, her green eyes catching me staring. I sputtered as she approached and continued to act like a complete circus clown when she placed the cup of tea she poured in front of me, sliding it closer to my side of the table.

"Here we go, dear," she said warmly. "Double cream Early Gray. Your usual."

My heart jolted. In all my years in Orchard Hollow, I had not had any place I visited often enough to have a usual anything. It was odd, but I really enjoyed the feeling of belonging that Edith provided with those simple words.

Smiling, I sniffed the sugary steam wafting from the cup, my shoulders relaxing. "Thank you, Edith. I sure needed this today."

The teashop owner's brows rose an inch higher.

"Oh?" she said. "Is everything all right at the funeral home?"

I pursed my lips into a tight line, acting as though I was hesitant to speak. In truth, this was exactly what I came here for. If I wanted to know who Henry was arguing with, Mrs. Dawson would tell me. She made it her business to know everyone in the town—a fact I found out from Finn on the last case we worked together. Now all I had to do was make it seem that she was expertly sucking the information from me, and I would have her hooked.

Shifting my weight from one side to the other, I tightened my grip on the teacup, saying, "The funeral home is fine," I said. "It's me that's the problem. I can't get what happened to Henry out of my head."

"Yes, it was unbelievable, wasn't it? What a terrible accident."

Was it, though?

I cleared my throat. "So awful," I said. "I feel horrible for his friends and family."

"Well, Henry didn't have too many of those, I'm afraid."

"Really?" I asked, my voice rising in false surprise. "I

thought with the turnout at the event that he was quite popular."

Edith waved her hand in front of her face. "Nonsense. Those were nothing but nosy townsfolk eager to get the latest story. You can't whisper the word treasure in a place like ours without the entire town showing up." She sniffled, folding her arms over her large chest. "I bet you half the people there didn't even like poor old Henry. Or were jealous of his career. It is quite the adventure to devote your life to chasing treasure."

"I got the impression that Henry was more interested in the ship than what was on board," I said. "But I see your point. Come to think of it, I saw him arguing with a woman not a few days before the event. Maybe she was one of the people you mentioned."

The apron Mrs. Dawson wore crinkled as she moved in closer to me. "That must have been Clara," she said matter-of-factly. "Those two hadn't seen eye to eye in ages."

"Clara? I don't think I know her."

The teashop owner pulled up an empty chair and settled in. Her elbows rested on the table, and she placed her chin into the palms of her hands, her eyes twinkling with mischief. "Clara Blythe," she announced. "Henry and she were a pair in high school. Lovebirds, if you get my drift."

I think everyone gets your drift, Edith.

I nodded. "I take it they didn't end on good terms?"

"Not even remotely. It was all the news back in the day when they split up," Mrs. Dawson said. "They would be seen yelling at each other for months after it happened. It was probably something to do with the repair shop they co-owned. I always tell people, never mix business with pleasure. When the pleasure ends, the business suffers."

Glaring at her, I took a sip of the warm tea and asked, "Henry owned a repair shop?"

"Ha! Sort of. That man was always chasing one dream or another," the teashop owner replied. "When he went off to study history, leaving Clara alone to run the shop, I was certain he'd be back with another big dream idea of his. But it seemed he was bitten by the history bug. The two broke up not long after he started his studies, and Clara took over the shop. Has been running it on her own ever since."

The tea got lodged in my throat, my body stilling. I pierced the teashop owner with a serious gaze. "What kind of repairs does Clara do?"

"Anything you can imagine. If it's broken, that woman can fix it," Edith said. "But her specialty is electronics. You know, if you saw them arguing, it was likely about the event."

"Why do you say that?"

One of the women called out for Mrs. Dawson and

she pushed her chair out, rising to stand. She raised a finger in the air to let the woman know she'd be by momentarily, then turned back to me. Her eyes narrowed. She pursed her lips, gaze flicking from the women to me.

"Clara was the one who set up the entire presentation," she said. "If not for her, Henry would have been up there with a chalkboard playing Pictionary and not flashing his fancy pictures for all to see." She sighed. "Though, all things considered, perhaps that would have had a better outcome for him in the end."

As she twirled on her heels and walked away, my mind clung to her last words, churning them over in my head. Mrs. Dawson didn't know how right she was. Henry's death could have been avoided if he hadn't used the faulty projector, but perhaps someone else already knew that. Perhaps they'd even planned it all along.

Clara Blythe's repair shop was more of a warehouse than a store. Located on a dark, narrow side street in a residential area twenty minutes from Cliff Row, it screamed "Enter at your own risk!" upon entrance.

I pushed open the rusted door, and the hinges squeaked to announce my entry. On my left, a ceiling-high wall shelf with a mish-mash array of wires and electronic parts obscured the better half of the small shop. It leaned slightly forward, and I found myself squeezing over to the right as I walked in case it toppled over and crushed me to death. A scrap of metal protruding from a basket caught my pants, making me jerk backward. I shook it loose, ignoring the tiny rip that now embellished my pants. The bright overhead lights lit up the space in a sterile and unwelcoming manner, and I narrowed my watery eyes as I looked around. Near the entrance, more shelves and workbenches sat haphazardly in the rectangular space. All were messy and full to the brim with tools, wires, and half-disassembled devices. Old monitors and vintage radios were stacked in one corner opposite a workbench, their power cords tangled on the side. The air had a faint smell of solder that made my stomach turn and my mouth dry up.

Taking a few careful steps inward, I listened to the sound of a soldering iron humming and followed it to a small table tucked behind a tall shelf. A magnifying lamp lit up a small figure hunched over at the table. I instantly recognized the woman as the same one I saw on the street with Henry.

Clara Blythe.

I approached slowly, my feet padding over the sticky linoleum floor. As I neared Clara, a fluff of orange fur zoomed by me and I gasped, grasping at my chest from the shock.

The woman stopped what she was doing, turning in

the chair to face me. Her eyes glinted in the light, and she darted them from me to the large orange tabby cat dashing across the shop floor. She rolled her eyes. "Felix! Stop hunting the customers." Her gaze landed on me. "Sorry about him. He still thinks he's a street cat, even though he's been spoiled rotten for years."

To prove her point, Clara slid open a desk drawer and pulled out a bag of cat treats, pouring a hefty amount into a bowl at her feet. The cat, Felix the Hunter, rushed toward the bowl in a flash and proceeded to empty it instantly. The sound of smacking gums and cat purrs filled the empty space between me and Clara.

I winced. "No need to apologize. I have a similar fiend at home," I said. Memories of Theo inhaling a bag of cut salami flashed before my eyes.

"So, you understand," Clara said. "My name is Clara, by the way. Now what can I help you fix? Broken cellphone? Laptop crashed? I got you covered."

My hands shot up. "Nothing like that, I'm afraid. Sorry if I gave you the wrong idea. My name is Lyra Moore. I was a ... friend of Henry Barlow's."

A darkness passed over Clara's features, but it was gone before it took root. She shook her head, her short curls bouncing around her shoulders.

"Henry never mentioned you."

"Maybe a friend is a stretch," I admitted. "I run the

funeral home up on the cliffs. Henry was a regular customer." When Clara's face scrunched in confusion, I added, "People like to get a head start sometimes. To plan their funeral."

The technician folded her arms into a pretzel. "And Henry was one of these people? Really?"

"Is that odd?"

She shrugged. "Honestly, with Henry, nothing was all that odd. I'm sure you gathered he was a bit of an eccentric. Always had been, even back when we were together." She looked me up and down. "I'm sorry. Why are you here exactly?"

Because I suspect you may have had a hand in his death.

I pressed my lips into a tight, thin line. "I wanted to speak to people close to him. Friends and family and such," I lied. "To see if anyone would like to speak at the ceremony."

"Oh, you don't want me doing that," Clara barked.

"I was told you two used to be a couple. I didn't mean to overstep, but I figured with your history you'd be a great fit to say a few words."

That darkness returned to her face and this time Clara didn't fight it. She slumped in the chair, pulling out a few more cat treats to add to Felix's bowl. The cat devoured them in moments.

"It isn't that," she finally said. "While I would love to help, I'm afraid I won't be coming to the funeral."

My brows hiked up to meet my hairline. "How come?"

"I'm not welcome," she said curtly. "Henry didn't have a lot of family, but the family he had ... Well, let's say they're the reason we are no longer together."

I swallowed the lump forming in my throat.

"I thought you broke it off after Henry went away to school."

Judging by the look on her face, the information was news to Clara. "We didn't. Henry and me, we were on and off for years after he returned to town. Whatever you may have heard, it's not true. We were good friends despite our relationship not working out."

"Then what happened? If you don't mind me asking."

Clara sighed. "Eloise Penrose happened," she said dimly. "Henry's niece. She weaseled her way into Henry's life after he started researching that stupid ship. Henry changed after that. *She* changed him."

"Changed him how?" I asked.

"For the worse," Clara replied. "He became obsessed with the ship, but I have the feeling that Eloise had a lot to do with it. She was his only heir, you see. Needless to say, if Henry found that blasted ship, she'd stand to inherit quite a bit of money if the rumors of the treasure were true."

My body stiffened, and I had to lean against the wall to appear less intrigued, so I didn't give myself away. This was the first I heard of a niece; Henry never mentioned Eloise in all the times he came by the funeral home. And to think she was his sole heir! My teeth split, jaw unhinging. *An inheritance could be enough to kill for.*

"Suspicious, isn't it?" Clara asked, noticing my gaping mouth. "The timing, I mean. The last time I spoke to Henry was only a few days before he died. That was when he told me he put Eloise in his will. That snake of a girl was going to get everything Henry worked his entire life for. I was furious with him."

That must have been the argument I witnessed. I kept my expression neutral when I asked, "Did you tell him how you felt?"

"Sure did! I never held back with Henry, not with our history. But he wouldn't hear a word of it."

"What did you do?"

She scoffed. "Told him he was on his own from then on. I didn't have the time to deal with his family drama. I had a business to run."

Tapping a finger to my chin, I glanced at the computer splayed into pieces on the desk behind her. "Since you're an expert in this, did you think it strange how Henry died? Do projectors usually electrocute people?"

"Anything with a charge can do that," Clara said. "But I checked that machine myself before I gave it to Henry, and it was in perfect condition. Maybe he dropped it when he was setting it up or something. Or someone else did. Whatever it was, it happened after I had my hands on it."

She looked over her shoulder and groaned. "Speaking of machines, unless you have a job for me, I should really get back to this," she said. "The bills don't pay themselves around here. *Some of us* have to work to keep the lights on."

The way she said those words made it obvious who she meant. My thoughts drifted to Henry's niece as I thanked the technician for her time and dodged Felix's paws on the way out of the shop. Outside, the sun had started to set, and the air filled with a new chillness that only an early spring evening could bring. I shivered, skirting around a turned over garbage can in the alley as I made my way back to the truck.

It was beginning to look as if Henry's life was far from the boring existence I thought him to have. Between the sunken treasure, the jaded ex, and the gold-digging niece, there was no shortage of reasons for someone to want the historian dead.

The name Eloise Penrose drifted through my brain

like a wave. At least now I was one step closer to narrowing down my search for a possible suspect.

I checked the time on my phone, the hairs rising on my arms as I hurried my step. I needed to chase down that lead, but first I had better return to the manor and feed Theo before he decided to make a point by shredding my couch again.

Chapter Nine

The manor was eerily quiet when I arrived. I stalked down the driveway, my eyes narrowing on every creeping shadow as I climbed up the front porch steps. For some reason, I couldn't shake the feeling that I was being watched. The hairs on the back of my neck stood up straight and my toes curled inside my boots.

I turned around, glancing around the front yard. It was completely empty save for my truck parked near the entrance. My neck turned to look toward the cliffs. The massive oak that teetered nearly at the edge stood stoically tall, its branches swaying in the light wind of the early evening. Beyond it, the sound of the sea crashing into the shore below filled my ears.

For a second, I thought I saw movement near one of

the large rocky walls that jutted out from the earth, but it was only a seagull zooming by. It dove out of sight, likely landing on the small beach at the lowest part of the property.

I shook my head, embarrassed by my own foolishness. Of course, no one was around. I was driving myself insane. That was all this was.

Rolling my shoulders into a rigid, straight line, I twirled back to face the front door and slid my key into the lock. The warmth of the house hit my face as soon as I opened the door and I smiled, the smell of the manor enveloping me in a cocoon of familiarity. I pulled off my boots and tossed the keys in the bowl on the side table before closing the locks and the door latch behind me. Then I set off in search of Theo.

It was bizarre not to see him at the door as soon as I arrived. I was a good thirty minutes late feeding him and the changeling never let me live down running behind. Not when food was involved.

"Theo!" I yelled, my sharp voice piercing the darkness of the manor like an arrow. "I'm home!"

Silence.

The quietness of the manor swallowed me whole. I paced further, and every step made me all the more nervous. The shutters on the windows slammed against the outside brick and my steps faltered from the sudden sound. I looked up at the swinging chandelier above my head, then darted my gaze to the winding staircase leading upstairs.

Did I leave a window open?

I was certain I didn't, but the slight whooshing of wind and the swinging chandelier made me reconsider. I checked the long, darkened hallway before spinning to the stairs and dashing to the second level of the house. Heart racing in the cage of my chest, I cleared the last two steps in one long stride and slid across the wood floor, my socks having no traction. Clumsily, I made my way from room to room, checking for the source of the draft.

After inspecting the bathroom and bedroom, I stopped short in front of one of the two guest rooms on this level of the manor. The window in the room was wide open. My stomach sank. I hadn't stepped foot in the guest rooms all week.

Panic rose up my body as I backed away from the open doorway, my shoulders slamming into the wall behind me. "Theo!"

I did not like where this was going. The eerie silence, the open window, it all pointed to bad news. And where was that Fairy-blasted cat?

I tore through the manor like a madwoman on a mission. Honestly, if this was a movie, I'd have a cloud of dust kicking up behind me with how fast I ran from room to room, from corner to corner, searching for Theo.

By the time I finished going through the entirety of the house, I was breathless and sweaty ... and still very much cat-less.

Terror ripped through me as I slid to a stop in front of the open back door. I walked slowly toward it, then paused again next to my gardening tools. Reaching for the trowel, I wrapped my fingers over the metal handle, then shook my head, putting the trowel down again. If this was who I thought it was, my makeshift weapon would be useless.

Eyes wide as saucers, I ripped off my sweater, skimming down to the tank top I had underneath. Then I dropped the illusion on my wings. They burst from my back and the relief that flowed through my body was enough to make me exhale the breath I was holding. Sparkles filled the air around me as my magic swirled over my body. My pearlescent skin caught the glimmer of the hallway lights and reflected them in rainbow glints on the floral wallpaper.

I bit the inside of my cheek and stepped outside.

The fairy magic I let loose did wonders to keep me warm, and I barely felt the cool air as it grazed my exposed skin, though the adrenaline coursing through my veins likely had a lot to do with it. I walked at a slow pace around the house and headed toward the garden. My eyes caught on a new boot print on the earth and my knees knocked. They were too big to be one of mine and since no one else came back here, it was clear now that I was right to worry. Someone had been to my home while I was away.

The panic ripped me to shreds inside as my mind created alternate scenarios of what could have happened. Was Rhyven waiting for me in the garden? Did he come alone, or did he cross into this realm with his royal guards?

I swallowed around the lump in my throat.

Did he hurt Theo?

In the distance, the garden came into view. My magic swirled faster around me and blocked the trail that led ahead. I swatted at it to clear my vision, but it was no use—my anxiety made it impossible to calm its wild energy.

Struggling to see clearly, I focused on the small bundle of a figure on the garden bench. My heart jolted as I neared the fluffy gray fur, and I ran the rest of the way to clear the distance between the bench and me.

I fell to my knees, sucking in a sharp breath.

"Theo? What are you doing out here?" I screeched. "Didn't you hear me calling you?"

The cat said nothing. His amber eyes flicked to me briefly before returning to their original focus point. Theo shook his head, his ears perked up high. He lifted a tiny paw and nudged it in the direction of the roses I had taken so much pride in.

I followed his gaze, my jaw hitting the ground.

"They're—"

"Purple," Theo said. "They changed color. How is that possible?"

A muscle in my neck feathered. "It wouldn't be," I replied. "Not unless someone did this."

"The Shadow Prince," Theo said. He stood up and walked to the other side of the bench, reaching down to pick something up with his teeth. Returning, he pried his mouth open, and a small envelope fluttered down between us. "He left you this."

Brow furrowed, I slipped my finger under the flap and tore it open to reach inside. My hands trembled as I pulled out the cream-colored paper tucked in the envelope. Unfolding it, I rolled my gaze over the careful script covering the page. My pulse skyrocketed and my lungs refused to expand. Color leached from my face as I reread the prince's words.

"What does it say?" Theo asked, jarring me from my stupor.

I gulped down air like it was water and I had been lost in the desert for days. Folding the page in half, I placed it back in the envelope and looked at the changeling.

"A word of advice," I read, trying not to attach Rhyven's voice to each word. "I'd keep a better eye on the cat. You don't want something to happen to him."

Next to me, Theo's jaw set. We gazed at each other —speechless. The Prince of the Shadow Court was not playing around. This was a threat, and the worst part was that I was no longer the only one in danger. I put Theo in the prince's path. My skin crawled. At my back, my wings fluttered, and I gritted my teeth in response.

I never thought that I would regret my choice to leave Fairy as much as I did now.

Chapter Ten

I tapped the edge of the teacup and reached for the tablet Rosemary held out. Turning the screen around, I scrolled through the information before me.

"This is interesting," I said.

Rosemary nodded. "I know. It's the first time I heard someone mention a second ship. Everyone seems focused on the Hollow Siren, so this came as a surprise."

I looked at the name attached to the article Rosemary found. "Everyone except Henry. You said you found the article on the university's website?"

"Sure did," Rosemary replied. "The historian was very well liked there. He had a few articles published by the university's press."

The sound of slurping and sighing made me turn my head toward Mortimer, who was enjoying a hot cup of tea beside me. He eyed the tablet in my hands with an amused expression. "Let me guess," Mortimer said. "The articles are all about the ship."

"Not all," Rosemary corrected. "Some are about the family that owned it."

Mortimer raised a brow, and she shrugged, defeated. It appeared that Mortimer had a good point—for all intents and purposes, Henry seemed to be obsessed with the Hollow Siren. I wondered what it was about it that made the historian so attached to the ship. I mean, sure, a treasure was exciting to study, but there were so many historical events in human history with mysterious pasts. Why focus on this one ship?

It was strange. Even for Henry.

I skipped ahead in the article, focusing on Rosemary again. "When did all these articles get published?"

She checked the notes she had made in a leather-bound journal and said, "Most came out in the last year or so. I can double-check when I get back to the funeral home. I left the rest of my notes with Ellie."

Mortimer and I exchanged twin looks of awe.

"You were researching this while your mom is visiting?" Mortimer asked.

Rosemary winced. "It was a good break from the

hectic energy back at home. And I couldn't leave Ellie to run the funeral home all on her own for so long," she explained. "What kind of business partner would I be if I did that?"

"Right, of course," Mortimer said. I noticed the pitch of his tone bordered on the skeptical and I had to agree. It was certain that Rosemary diving into researching a random death and burying herself in her work had a lot more to do with her needing a break from her mother than with Ellie requiring help. In the time I've known the two funeral home owners, I had yet to see Ellie requiring assistance. She was a force to be reckoned with.

I smiled at Rosemary, swallowing down the million questions I had. Family was a lot. I knew that better than anyone, and if Rosemary needed a break, then I was more than happy to provide it.

Putting the tablet down, I leafed open one of the books Mortimer had brought with him when the two Wardens came by this morning. The title page was promising, a bold script spelling out "Famous Disappearances in the West." The Hollow Siren was listed prominently in the third spot on the table of contents, and I quickly flipped the pages to reach the chapter that belonged to it. There were a good twenty pages devoted to the ship and several black and white photographs displayed throughout the dense text passages. I recognized one of the images as the photo of the ship that Henry opened his presentation with on the weekend. My heart stopped momentarily at the memory of the historian.

Shaking off thoughts of Henry, I put all my attention on the book splayed open on the coffee table in front of me. My legs tingled and I had to rearrange them, sitting up higher on my knees.

"Hmm," I mused as I read one passage.

Mortimer pulled his reading glasses down on his nose and looked down at the page. "Find anything interesting?"

"Maybe. This book says that the Whitmores were known for being secretive, going as far as to hire actors that resembled them to distract the public from themselves."

Mortimer's eyes crinkled at the corners. "I didn't realize they were so famous."

"Me neither," I agreed. "Although it's possible they were simply eccentric."

"I guess we'll never really know now," Rosemary said.

Frowning, I perused the rest of the article but wasn't able to unearth any more than we already knew. According to the historical papers we'd found, the Hollow Siren departed from the west coast on March

16th, just as Henry said it did. The two couples on board were experts in sailing and the men had even been known to dive in dangerous tides and beat some of the most extreme world records. The Whitmores' past made it all the more bizarre that they somehow managed to vanish in the water, though I supposed there was no messing with nature. The ocean took what the ocean wanted, or that was what Mortimer said when I told him about this part of the sordid tale.

Aside from the photograph taken not long before their departure, there were records of reports from the docks of crates being loaded onto the Hollow Siren the night prior. Some of the reports stated that the crates contained diving equipment and provisions, while others said they were full of gold and jewels. Considering the times and the little information we could gather about the ship; it was hard to establish the truth behind the words.

On that date of the year 1911, the ship set off in perfect weather. But less than a week later, a storm was said to have been spotted within the ship's original course, and it disappeared, never to be recovered. For decades, people speculated on what may have happened and the Hollow Siren attracted a sort of cult following of historians that all wished to uncover the truth. No one did. Of course.

The mysterious aura surrounding the ship was

infectious, and I found myself getting dragged into the stories, making my own speculations about what may have occurred.

I was in the midst of one of these theories when a loud knock startled me back to the room. I glanced from Rosemary to Mortimer, asking, "Were Finn and Ellie planning to stop by?"

"Not that I know of," Rosemary said. "Ellie is knee-deep in paperwork back at the funeral home."

"And Finn is doing a double shift at the hospital," Mortimer said. "Apparently their head mortician quit, so he has to fill in."

Grimacing, I stood up and walked out of the living room, taking a sharp right toward the front door. On the way, I passed by Theo, who was too busy polishing off a bowl of whipped cream to notice me. The rascal was going to pay for that later. Cats may not be allergic to the stuff like changelings were in human form, but no one could handle that much dairy without conse-quences. I rolled my eyes, preparing for a night of caring for the furry troublemaker while he spent hours with an upset stomach.

Padding past the kitchen, I neared the front door and rose on my tippy toes to peer through the small window in its center. My heart rate slowed. It was only the mailman.

I opened the door gingerly, a wide smile stretching my lips.

"Hi, Danny."

The mailman grinned. "Hey, Lyra. Got something for you," he said, handing me a small package wrapped in brown packing paper. "Needs a signature."

I eyed the package. For the life of me, I couldn't remember ordering anything recently. Most of the supplies for the morgue had already arrived earlier this week, and I confiscated my credit card from Theo after I caught him ordering ten large pizzas on a random Tuesday. *I wonder what it is.*

Signing for the delivery, I thanked Danny and waited until he drove off to rip into the package. Under the paper was a slim notebook with a leather cover and a long leather string that wrapped around it several times. Slowly, I unwrapped the string, my eyes widening as I read the name scratched into the front page. Shutting the door behind me, I returned to the living in complete stupor. The manor drifted by me in a blur and when I reached the others, I had forgotten they were there at all.

"What do you have there?" Mortimer asked.

I swallowed hard, my pulse hammering between my temples. Fingers slick with sweat, I put the notebook on the coffee table, taking a step backward. "It's Henry's journal," I answered. "I think he sent it to me before he died."

"Why would he do that?"

Shivers tripped down my spine. "I have no idea," I admitted. "But if he sent this to me, then it could only mean one thing. Henry Barlow knew he was in danger, and he needed to keep this notebook safe. Whatever is in here, it could be the key to solving his murder."

Chapter Eleven

Henry's notebook was more locked up than a Swiss bank vault. Every page was written in some sort of code that none of us could decipher. There were combinations of numbers jotted on every page that interfered with the hand scribbled text, making it impossible to make sense of anything inside. I had no idea that Henry was this secretive, but the notebook proved me wrong. I turned the book sideways, inspecting the long line of numbers under a sketch of the ship.

We were not going to get anywhere at this rate.

"I don't get it," I told the others. "Why send the notebook to me without instructions on how to read it?"

Rosemary frowned, the lines around her full lips

creasing deeply. "I agree. Especially since you said the two of you weren't all that close."

Sitting on the couch with Theo nestled beside him, Mortimer harrumphed before picking up the notebook. His pale eyes studied the numbered passages, and he flipped the pages back and forth, a glimmer of understanding flashing in his serious gaze.

Hope fluttered in my chest.

"You need a cipher code," Mortimer announced.

My previous hope burst into flames and sizzled out. I looked at the mortician. "Any chance you know what it is?"

"It's not so simple. A cryptogram—which is what this certainly is—requires a code that only the writer of the puzzle knows," Mortimer said. "Once you have the key code, the rest should fall into place fairly simply."

I looked at the text on the page as Mortimer put the notebook back on the table between us. Some of the numbers were punctuated by small crosses, like one would find in multiplication tables. The cipher wasn't mathematical though, we had already tried that route and got nowhere.

My shoulders dropped down into a slouch. "There is nothing simple about Henry, I'm afraid." I pointed to a passage written on one page. "What do you think this means?"

"The riddle?"

Mortimer shrugged, putting on his reading glasses. He cleared his throat and brushed down the vest of his four-piece suit before beginning to read. My smile widened at his booming voice. You'd have thought the man was a theater performer in a past life.

"Beneath the waters where shadows sleep,
Lies a secret the tides cannot keep.
A vessel of splendor, with riches untold,
Sails never feeling the wind's biting cold.
Her sister, a trickster, danced the sea,
A voyage made for all to see.
But among the sailors, bold and true,
The treasure waits, disguised from view."

I glanced at Rosemary, her grin matching mine.

"Fascinating stuff," Mortimer said. "And very cryptic."

"It has to be about the ship," Rosemary said.

I mouthed the words to myself, repeating the riddle in my head until I had it memorized. *What were you trying to tell me, Henry?* My attention caught on the second passage, and I gasped. "Should we look into the sister-in-law?"

When the Wardens didn't respond and only looked at me in confusion, I said, "The part about the sister dancing in the sea. Henry said that Percival Whitmore traveled with his brother and his wife. The sister in the sea could be her."

"Hmm. It's possible," Rosemary whispered. "I can see what I can dig up about her when I get home."

I instantly thought of her mother. "Shouldn't you be—"

"Not at all," Rosemary cut me off curtly.

I winced.

Luckily, Mortimer was not about to let me dig myself into a hole with all the questions I had for the funeral home owner. He stood up and stalked past us, ignoring Theo's disapproving glare after being woken up. The taupe fabric of his suit glimmered in the light streaming in from the bay window, and he looked as dapper as ever as he turned to gaze at me over his shoulder.

The mortician nudged his chin toward the door. "In the meantime, perhaps Lyra and I can take another route," he said.

"What are you plotting?"

Mortimer's thick gray brows wiggled. "I think it's time we followed the money," he said before twirling on his heels and storming out of the room.

All curiosity was thrown aside when I realized Mortimer meant Henry's money and not the fruitless treasure hunt we were on. We stood on the opposite side of the street, our eyes glued to the small bungalow Eloise Penrose had rented several months ago. It was a fine enough place, but it lacked any personality. Unlike the other homes on the quiet residential street not far from the beach, the bungalow was painted a boring gray. Not pink or purple or turquoise, like every other home that sandwiched it on either side. There was no greenery in the front yard except for a small tree that appeared to have been dead for quite some time. Even the fence that once surrounded the property was down to only pegs. I glanced at the windows with blinds drawn down and grimaced. If Eloise planned to stay indefinitely to be with her uncle, this was the last place I'd have expected her to rent out. After all, there were much better options closer to town and to Henry, who lived a good forty-minute drive from this location.

I side glanced Mortimer. "How did you know she was renting here?"

"What do you think?"

I chuckled. Of course, he got his information from the town's snoop librarian. I was starting to think that Maggie Halloway knew so much about everyone in town because of her innate need for information and not for the supposed book she was writing. I mean, why would she even know where Eloise was staying or who she was? Granted, Henry's death probably set her off. Not that I could blame her, it set me off as well.

I had to admit, Mortimer's relationship with the woman had saved us on more than one occasion so far. It was truly nice to have her on our side.

The front door of the bungalow swung open, and I froze. Beside me, Mortimer readjusted his bowler hat and said, "We're up."

I followed him across the street, the toe of my boot getting caught on the sidewalk on the other side. I stumbled with a loud, panicked gasp, righting myself moments before I face planted on the yellowing dry grass of Eloise's front lawn. My magnificent display of agility caught her attention, and her eyes rolled over Mortimer and me in suspicion.

"Excellent entrance," Mortimer said jovially.

My cheeks burned with the heat of the earth's core.

"Hi there!" Mortimer said cheerfully, closing the distance between himself and Eloise in a few long strides. She backed away slightly as he extended a hand in greeting. "Are you by any chance Eloise Penrose?"

The unease flowing off the young woman was palpable. She tilted her head to the side, the puffy bun on her head sliding over. Eloise rearranged it to sit even higher and pushed her thick-framed cats-eye glasses up on her sharp nose. Her hazel eyes tracked my movements as I approached, in the same way Theo watched me when I brought home bacon.

"I am," she answered. "If you're selling something, I'm not interested."

Mortimer scuffed the bottom of his shoes on the single step leading to the makeshift front porch. He worked at a smile, but it faltered, and I watched Eloise frown when she noticed it.

The mortician was not the least bit deterred by her obvious annoyance with our presence there.

"Nothing like that, no," he said, waving her off. "We're here about your uncle, Henry Barlow." He nudged my side. "Lyra is in charge of his funeral arrangement, and we were hoping to get more information from a family member."

That seemed to do the trick. Eloise bristled before saying, "Oh. Why didn't you say so right away? I hadn't realized my uncle had arrangements made for his funeral."

Another nudge from Mortimer made me jump. I gritted my teeth, not enjoying having to lie to the woman one bit. It was one thing to pry information from an ex but something about lying to a family member after a death felt icky. And I knew a lot about liars. I did grow up in Fairy after all.

Shaking my head, I tamped down my doubts and told myself it was for the greater good.

"Your uncle had most of the details figured out and planned for over a year," I said. "But with the death being so sudden, we didn't get to finalize everything."

"Right. Yes, it was very unexpected. What did you need to know? I'll try to help as best I can."

Nodding, I tried to recall which pieces of the ceremony Henry left out, finally thinking of one. "The flowers," I blurted out. "Do you happen to know which flowers your uncle liked most? I can order them in for the wreath later this week."

"That's easy," Eloise said. "Henry loved daisies. He said they were beautiful in their simplicity."

Wow. For someone who was supposedly after Henry's money, Eloise sure knew her uncle. I couldn't pinpoint my father's favorite flower if my life depended on it, and I lived in his castle for most of my life.

Perhaps Henry's ex was wrong.

"It helped that daisies were Isadora Whitmore's flower of choice too," Eloise said suddenly. "Rumor has it she had buckets of them on board the ship when it went down."

I felt the light kick of Mortimer's shoe against my boot. What an odd thing to say. Even with her uncle's obsession with the ship, why mention it now? Unless her uncle wasn't the only one that fostered an unhealthy appetite for all things Hollow Siren. Was it possible they bonded over their mutual interest?

Or did Eloise know about the ship for other reasons?

Before I could ask her about it, the young woman groaned, drawing my attention back to her.

"I'm so sorry, but I'm running late for a meeting," she said, waving her phone in the air. "I can stop by tomorrow to answer any other questions you might have. I would like to make sure my uncle's service is exactly how he wished for it to be."

Knots twisted up my stomach. I smiled through them, reaching into my purse to pull out a business card. "Of course," I said. "Please call ahead when you think you'll be by so I can make sure to be there. And thank you, I appreciate the help."

"Anything for family," Eloise said.

She locked the door and the three of us marched down the street together in silence until we reached the rental car parked on the same block. The car, much like the house, was a boring gray with no frills. It drew so little attention to itself that I didn't realize it was parked there when we walked right by it earlier. Most of the tourists visiting our town came in flashy vehicles and rented the biggest houses closest to the water. Or maybe one of the more off the grid options up in the cliffs.

Not Eloise.

If I had to guess, I'd say that the woman wanted to disappear while she was here. I pushed the thought away. I had no reason to suspect Eloise.

And yet, why did I get such a strong dislike for her almost immediately?

Mortimer had the same notion, because when we climbed into the truck the first thing he told me was that we had to look into her more thoroughly. I agreed, starting the engine. I was already pulling into the street when my phone buzzed on the dashboard.

Placing the truck back in park, I checked the screen, a message bubble popping up. My gaze narrowed.

"What is it?" Mortimer asked, his intrigue mirroring my own.

I puckered my lips, flipping the screen to show him the message. "Rosemary thinks she cracked the riddle," I said.

As we made our way back to Mistbrook Manor, I couldn't help but smile. Finally, a break. Fairy knew I needed some good news for a change.

Chapter Twelve

The riddle was not what we thought. At all. While we still had no idea what the cipher code was and there was a good chance we would never figure it out, Rosemary was able to decipher the vague poem jotted down in full in Henry's notebook. Well, Rosemary with the Finn's help.

It was why I now sat opposite the hospital morgue director in the secret library beneath the mausoleum instead of being cozy at home. The entire situation was extra awkward because Rosemary sent him in her place and Mortimer conveniently had to dash out, leaving us alone in the quiet space. On any other day, I wouldn't mind being alone with Finn one bit, would welcome it, actually. But after the last warning from Rhyven, my mind was on anything but the romantic entanglement

I'd gotten myself into with the morgue director. I really should have stuck to my original plan and kept to myself.

"I think there is a good chance we're correct," Finn said.

I pushed my shoulder blades into the back of the chair, putting a sliver of more space between us. "I have to admit," I said. "I never considered that the Hollow Siren wasn't the only ship."

"But it makes sense, right? We're not grabbing at straws?"

The words of the riddle stared back at me from the whiteboard Finn dragged into the room. I studied the sentences, the meaning behind the words clearer now. "It appears to be the right direction," I said. "The part about the trickster sister dancing in the water makes a lot more sense now. If the sister was another ship, then it would stand to reason the Siren may be somewhere where no one else looked for it before."

"A decoy ship," Finn whispered.

I nodded. "Much like the actors the Whitmores used. Think about it—if you wanted to divert attention from what you were doing, what better way than to throw suspicion elsewhere?"

"The Whitmores could have sent the second ship out in the dead of night, making everyone believe it was the Siren," Finn agreed. "Then made off on the main ship. But where did they go?"

The words floated before my eyes in a jumbled mess. I pushed them aside mentally, pulling in a word at a time so I could make sense of the riddle. Now that we had an idea of what it meant, it was much easier to figure out the rest. My jaw unlocked and my tongue swelled in my mouth.

I got it!

My head swung around to face Finn. "Perhaps nowhere at all," I said.

"What do you mean?"

I stood up and walked to the whiteboard. Using a marker, I underlined the lines that mentioned the wind. Then the passage that talked about sailors. *Among the sailors, bold and true, the treasure waits, disguised from view.*

"I don't think the Hollow Siren sailed out," I announced. "I think this riddle is trying to tell us that the Whitmores hid it in plain sight. This whole time everyone had been looking for the decoy ship while the real one was sitting around somewhere, safe and sound."

Finn's lips twisted into a knot. "To think the treasure was in town this entire time," he breathed out. "Where would they hide a ship, though? At the docks?"

"No way. Too obvious," I replied. "They went to a lot of trouble with the spectacle. Wherever the ship is, it is well hidden. So well that no one had stumbled onto it in decades."

"I'm pretty sure Henry figured it out too," Finn said. "He possibly even went as far as to find out where to look. Or at least got close to it. It would explain why his notes are written in code. Something like the location of the Hollow Hoard would need protecting, especially if he thought he was in danger."

I shivered. "If that's true, then someone else knew what Henry found out. We were right all along. It was no accident that killed Henry—it was whoever was after what he knew. But how did they access the projector?"

Thinking for a moment, Finn held up a finger, saying, "That's our next move. We need to get a list of everyone that had access to the room the presentation was in and the projector."

"You can do that," I said. "I'm going to follow up on the people who might have interest in the treasure and were close to Henry."

"How will you do that?"

I glanced at the time on the clock hanging on the wall. A few more hours until the sun set and the day ended, then not long until morning came.

Pressing my lips tightly together, I looked at Finn. "I'm going to get real close to his only heir," I said. "And lucky for us, she's coming to Mistbrook first thing tomorrow."

The night passed in a sweaty blur dotted by terrorizing dreams of Rhyven and Fairy. When I woke up to the raging sound of the alarm clock, the sun was barely rising and my head pounded like drums at a rock concert. Groggily, I climbed out of my sweat-soaked bed and made my way to the bathroom, downing aspirin with water from the tap to make the headache lessen. It wouldn't do much good since my fae blood made me immune to human medicine, but the placebo effect still made me feel better so it was worth it.

After splashing some more water on my face, I headed downstairs, finding Theo in his usual corner of the couch, fast asleep.

Ah. To sleep like a changeling would be a blessing.

I tiptoed around the passed-out cat, carefully picking up the chocolate wrappers tossed on the floor from one of Theo's late-night movie binge sessions. Strange. I hadn't even heard him down here last night. I must have been more tired than I thought.

Continuing to clean up after the ratty creature, I put on a pot of tea and washed a few berries I picked up from the farmer's market two days ago. The fruit's flavor exploded in my mouth and I leaned against the counter, gazing out the kitchen window as the sun rose up over the cliffs. Gold and red hues painted the front yard in their sparkling tints and I felt every bone in my body turn to liquid when the rays of the sun hit my body. My gaze flicked to the row of herbs planted on the windowsill. I put the bowl of berries down and walked toward the plants, fairy magic coursing in my blood and tingling on my fingertips. Holding my palm over the green leaves, I let the magic drip from within me and into the herbs. Glitter fell onto the leaves in an array of colors. I smiled, watching the herbs grow an inch taller in return.

I must have been standing there for longer than I realized because before I knew it, there was a knock on the front door that reverberated through the entire manor. I jumped, the sound jarring me.

On the way to the door, I checked the grandfather clock, my pulse speeding up and the throbbing behind my temples increasing when I saw what time it was. I was so out of it I completely forgot that Eloise was supposed to stop by at eight this morning. And it was already half past.

Gliding to a stop in front of the large door, I unlocked the three main locks and slid the chain off before opening. My heart leaped into my chest when I saw who was standing on the other side.

"You're not Eloise," I blurted out.

The man in front of me cocked a single bushy brow and flashed his pearly white teeth at me. The smell of his cologne filled my nostrils, and I tried not to gag on reflex. It was a disturbing combination of musk and mint that did not sit well with my stomach. As the man extended a rough, tanned hand, I battled the urge not to slam the door in his face.

"No, I am not. I'm afraid she had another meeting to take, but she sent me in her place," the man said. "My name is Duncan Price. I'm Eloise's boyfriend."

Sparks of recognition ignited in my brain, but no matter how hard I tried, I couldn't place why this man seemed so familiar. I was certain I'd met him before and yet I had no idea where or when. It was the strangest thing, since I usually had a good sense of people.

The man, Eloise's alleged boyfriend, glared at me across the threshold. My legs stood rooted in place and though I was ready to entertain Henry's niece, I had no intention of letting this stranger into my home.

I forced a calm expression to my scrunched-up face. "Nice to meet you," I said through gritted teeth. "Eloise didn't mention a boyfriend when I spoke with her. Are you staying in town, too?"

"I'm afraid not. I came down for a few days from the city after what happened to Henry." He reached into his pocket and produced a file folder, handing it to me. "Speaking of which, Eloise asked me to give this to you."

I took the folder, my fingers slick with sweat on top of the cream cardstock. "What is it?"

"A few of her instructions for the funeral," Duncan said. "She said you needed details for the ceremony."

I needed to find out if she killed her uncle, I thought, my jaw clenching tighter.

"I was hoping to speak to her in person," I said. "Do you know if she'd be able to stop by later today? Or I can come to her if that's easier."

Duncan's face paled slightly. "I can check, but no promises. She's quite busy. And I might be heading out myself soon," he answered. His blue eyes sparkled flirtatiously. "A shame I can't help you out. I only knew Henry professionally, so I doubt I'd have much to offer in this case."

"Oh? Were you a historian as well?" I asked. "Or did you know him from college?"

"Good lord, no!" Duncan exclaimed. "I fancy myself a bit of a treasure hunter, so our paths have crossed before. Only briefly, of course."

For a second, when he took a few steps toward me, I thought he was going to try to force his way into the house. But Duncan stopped a few inches from me and leaned in, the coffee smell on his breath lingering between us. He licked his bottom lip, whispering, "Don't tell Eloise this, but I always thought her uncle was ... How can I put it? A madman. Chasing tales of treasures instead of concentrating on more serious work. Some historian, huh?"

I closed the door an inch.

"Didn't you say you were a treasure hunter?"

Duncan chuckled and raked his fingers through his blond hair. "I sure did. The difference is, I didn't waste four degrees to become one."

I was starting to get the distinct feeling that Duncan and Henry did not get along, and I was willing to bet Eloise was at the center of the feud. In all honesty, I was on Henry's side, despite not knowing what it was. Something about Duncan made my blood run cold—I didn't trust the man farther than I could throw him, and judging by his refrigerator-shaped physique, it wasn't very far at all.

I leaned against the doorframe, blocking the view of the manor from his sightline.

"Well, I think Henry had a lot to offer," I said defensively. "And the story of the Hollow Siren is very famous around these parts. I wouldn't go around saying anything contrary if I were you; you never know how people might react."

A loud, boisterous laugh fell from Duncan's lips at my words. The sound of it grated on my nerves and my mind spun as flashes of its memory attacked my system. I stifled a gasp.

That's where I know you from!

I knew I saw Duncan before and that laugh confirmed it. He was the same man we saw waiting in line at the Whistling Kettle. The one who was wrapped around that flashy-dressed woman who was most definitely not Eloise. My eyes narrowed on Duncan when I asked, "How long have you and Eloise been dating?"

"Ages," he replied. "I'm kidding. But it has been a few years now. Getting very serious."

You lying, cheating scumbag.

I bit down on my tongue to avoid saying anything else. The sleazeball on my doorstep didn't know that I saw him that day, and to keep things less complicated, I needed to stay silent. There was no point in getting involved in Eloise's romantic life. I looked at the treasure hunter with an angry gaze. What if Henry found out that Duncan was cheating on his niece? If things were serious as the treasure hunter said, and if he knew Eloise was going to inherit all of Henry's money, it could be reason enough to want her uncle dead. Was it possible that Duncan wasn't only a terrible person but also a killer?

I took a wavering step backward, closing the door another inch.

"I should probably let you go," I said, hiding the panic in my voice. Raising the folder, I waved it between us. "Thank you for bringing this by."

"No trouble at all."

He flashed me a winning smile that made acid shoot up my throat. Taking another step into the manor, I waved goodbye and shut the door, then locked it. My fingers curled around the file folder, creasing it so deeply I was sure it would be impossible to read what was written inside. Prying the curtains of the window beside the door open, I watched Duncan climb into a bright red sports car, his shiny loafers kicking up the pebbles in my driveway.

The first thing I did after Duncan drove out of sight was pick up my laptop and get to work on finding out everything I could about the man. Cheating was unfortunately not a crime punishable by the law, but murder? That was another story altogether.

Chapter Thirteen

Finding information on Duncan was the easiest thing I had to do in a while; the man loved attention, and his face was plastered on every social media website and several online articles. Unfortunately, there was nothing that pointed to him having any motive for wanting Henry dead. Except for the cheating, Duncan appeared to be a pretty stand-up individual.

Yet I didn't buy it.

I wasn't sure what it was, but there was an air about him that reminded me of my father—an arrogance that clung to him like an old cologne gone sour. It wasn't only the way he carried himself, shoulders squared, but the sharp, blatant stench of a man who thought only of himself. The kind of presence that left a room colder when he walked away.

With a groan, I shut the laptop, the dull click of the lid snapping shut louder in the silence than I expected. Sliding my forearms across the morgue desk, the polished surface was cool against my skin. My toes curled, muscles tingling, as I stretched my back into something resembling a straight line. I had been sitting in the downstairs office chair so long that the wood felt like an extension of me, its hard edges pressing familiar grooves into my skin.

The old stairs creaked, the sound slicing through the hush in a warning. I glanced up, my tired eyes meeting Theo's furry face where he peeked through the doorway at the top. Framed by the golden light spilling from the upper level, his silhouette took on an ethereal glow, his long whiskers catching the sun enough to make them shimmer. For a moment, he looked almost like a tiny, benevolent spirit, come to check on me from some celestial plane. An angel, if angels had tufted ears and an unshakable belief in their own importance.

"It reeks of death here," Theo remarked. "If you want the Shadow Court Prince to leave you alone, all you have to do is bring him down here. He'll change his mind about marrying you real quick."

I frowned. Wasn't Lucifer an angel in human stories? Perhaps that was closer to the type of winged creature Theo was. My brows knitted close together. "What do you want, Theo?"

"You have visitors," the cat said.

"Really? Who?"

He shrugged, then licked the back of his paw, rolling his eyes at me. "How should I know?"

"Well, how did you know that someone was here?"

"I am a cat, Lyra," Theo said. "I may not be able to see through doors, but I am not deaf. Two cars pulled up a few minutes ago."

Hmm. I didn't have any appointments today. In fact, there were no appointments for the next few weeks, which, I supposed, considering the business I was in, was a good thing. I double checked to make certain I didn't forget anyone and confirmed that the day was clear.

Who was at the door, then?

I plugged the laptop in to charge and hauled myself up the stairs after Theo. Outside, the oval window of the front door was lit up in bright, colorful flashing lights. My stomach dropped when I realized who was likely waiting on the other side.

Tipping my chin down at Theo, I stopped in front of the door, my fingers hovering above the handle. "Why didn't you say it was the police?"

"It must have slipped my mind," the changeling said.

Somehow, I highly doubted that. Knowing Theo, it made his day to see me sweat when I realized the cops were here. What a brat.

I brushed back the frizzy hairs framing my face and opened the door. The shock of seeing Sheriff Romero on my doorstep was only mildly lessened by the other two people on the porch. I rose on my tiptoes to peer over the sheriff's wide-brimmed hat at Finn and Ellie.

"Hello, everyone," I said with a shaky voice. "What brings you all by?"

Sheriff Romero tipped his hat my way. "Afternoon, Lyra," he said. "I can't speak for your friends, but I am here to drop something off."

He bent down to pick up the box I hadn't noticed at his feet and handed it to me. I took it hastily, the weight of the items inside making my spine curve. The box was a simple thing with thick cardboard walls and the stamp of the Orchard Hollow Police Force on the lid.

I crooked a brow at the sheriff. "What's this now?"

"Henry Barlow's clothes from the day of the presentation," he said. "His niece said she'd like to bury him in the suit."

A low growl rumbled in my chest. "She could have dropped it off herself. I still need a few details from her for the funeral."

The sheriff's hands shot up in surrender, palms open, fingers splayed as if to ward off a blow. His boots scraped against the porch as he stumbled a step backward, his movements slow, deliberate—like someone easing away from a cornered animal. A flicker of uncertainty crossed his face, the briefest hesitation before he caught himself, schooling his expression into something more controlled. "I'm afraid I can't say anything to that," he said. Tipping his hat again, this time at the Wardens, he walked down the steps. When he reached the bottom, he turned around, his eyes sharp and pointed. "Don't forget to empty out the pockets. People always forget about those."

With that, he spun on his heels and marched to the police cruiser. As the sheriff rolled away and the lights extinguished from the front yard, I looked at Finn and Ellie. "That was odd," I said.

"Very suspicious," Finn agreed.

Before I could ask them why they stopped by, Ellie leaped for me, her fingers prying the box lid open. I shrieked, tumbling back.

"Ellie! What are you doing?"

Confusion painted her face a deeper shade of red. "Checking the pockets," Ellie said, as though it was the most obvious thing in the world. "Don't you want to know what he meant?"

Finn shook his head and rubbed his temples.

"I didn't realize he meant anything by it," I admitted.

Ellie guffawed. "Amateurs. The sheriff was clearly trying to tell you something. You need to read between the lines." She dug around the box, pushing Henry's suit every which way. A second later, she fished her arm out and held it up high. "Ta-da!"

Shifting closer to Finn, I cocked my head to the side to look at what she found. In Ellie's hand, the shine of metal reflected the sunlight, sparks of lights flashing over the manor's dark brick as she moved her hand. I leaned in. "What is that?"

"House keys," Ellie said. She dangled the ring of keys in front of our faces. "I think."

Snatching them from her, I turned the keys around. There were three keys in total. Two smaller ones and one that reminded me of the key I used to lock the front door of the manor. Ellie was right. These were definitely house keys. I touched the metal emblem of a ship dangling from the keychain; the initials H.B. etched into the sails. My throat was suddenly dry.

I swallowed, barely. "I think these might be Henry's keys," I said. "Why would the sheriff want me to have them?"

"You can't be that blind," Ellie scoffed. Then, looking at Finn, added, "You too. He obviously wants you to go there to see what you can find out. Didn't you say the sheriff all but told you to investigate the death yourself?"

"I suppose. I didn't believe he was serious."

Ellie took the keys back, shoving them in her pocket. "Clearly, he was. Let's get a move on."

I stood stock still, Finn refusing to budge beside me, while Ellie dashed toward his car parked in the driveway.

"She must be joking," I said.

Finn closed his eyes. "I'm afraid not. Believe it or not, she dragged me over here to convince you to break into the man's house. It appears now there is no excuse not to follow her wild plans."

I let out a slow, painful breath through clenched teeth. "What are the chances of talking her out of it?"

The honk of the car pierced the silence surrounding the manor as Ellie laid on it with all her force. She rolled down the window, her arm waving maniacally to beckon us over.

My chest contracted.

"Does that answer your question?" Finn asked, leaving me on the porch to join Ellie in the car.

Glancing up at the clear skies above, I rolled my shoulders, the sudden warmth in the air mellowing my anxious mood. Ugh. I supposed it was as good a day as any to break into a dead man's home. What else was new these days?

Chapter Fourteen

We arrived in front of a tidy little Craftsman home with a wraparound porch and a well-manicured lawn, the kind of place that should have felt inviting if not for the small fact that its only inhabitant was no longer alive. The house stood at the end of a quiet, tree-lined street, its deep green exterior blending into the landscape. A thick carpet of grass covered the walkway, damp from last night's rain, and the scent of wet earth lingered in the crisp air. The porch light was on, casting a glow over the steps that fought against the lessening daylight— weathered in a comfy lived-in sort of way.

The house itself was a classic, with a low-pitched roof and wide eaves, the kind of home built to last. An oak door sat framed between two leaded-glass windows, each one etched with a diamond pattern that reflected the rays of the sun that shone through the tree in the front yard. I imagined Henry standing there once, fussing with his keys, balancing an armful of books—never suspecting that one day it would be his last to do so.

To the right of the door, a rocking chair sat stiffly on the porch, the cushions slightly sun-faded. A porch swing hung further down, its chain rusty and creaking in the breeze. Closer to us, overgrown hedges lined the fence, and I caught a glimpse of a statue—something classical, maybe Greek or Roman—half-hidden in the lush greens.

I hesitated at the gate, the weight of what we were about to do settling in my chest. "Are we sure about this?" I asked, glancing at my partners in a possible crime.

Ellie, ever the pragmatist, adjusted the strap of her tiny backpack and shot me a look. "You were the one who wanted answers."

She had a point.

Beside her, Finn fidgeted with the cuff of his sweater, his eyes darting to the windows. "This feels like breaking and entering."

"It's not," I assured him, although I wasn't so sure myself. "The sheriff wanted me to check it out. I know that now. Otherwise, he wouldn't have given me Henry's keys."

"It still feels wrong," he muttered.

Ellie ignored both of us and pushed open the gate. It creaked loudly, the sound sending cold tremors down my arms. She turned to look at me over her shoulder. "Well, we didn't come all this way to stand on the side-walk. Let's get inside before someone notices."

I took a breath and followed them up the steps, steeling myself. The truth was in there somewhere. I just wasn't sure I wanted to find it. The more we uncovered about Henry's sordid past, the deeper we dug ourselves into the investigation. I knew the Grimm Wardens made it their life mission to solve crimes the police couldn't—or wouldn't, as it was in this case—but the idea of going down that route with them again made my skin prickle. Mostly because of how much I would miss them if I had to leave town, as I suspected I might. I had been teetering between staying and going for days now, with no real solution in sight. Perhaps I was kidding myself and simply prolonging the inevitable.

I bit the inside of my cheek as I watched Finn's broad back fill up the porch. Out of all the Wardens, I'd miss him most.

Tapping her foot impatiently, Ellie stretched out her hand, saying, "Do you have the keys?"

I handed the key set over reluctantly but said

nothing despite the rattling in my brain that told me to run. By now, I was used to living in fear and today was no different. Except this time, I didn't have an excuse not to push through it; not without aggravating Ellie, who was so excited for the chance to snoop it was bubbling out of her. The woman was seriously committed to solving the puzzle of Henry's death.

She pushed the largest of the keys into the bronze lock and twisted. My heart twisted with the key. The sound of the door creaking open pierced my ears, and I turned around to check the quiet street to make sure we were alone. The last thing we needed was for someone to call the police on three strangers going into a dead man's home. Something told me that just because the sheriff handed me the keys to Henry's house, didn't mean that he did so with the intention of the entire town knowing about it.

The smell of musty air burned my nostrils as the door swung open. The entryway opened into a narrow hall lined with bookshelves that drooped under the weight of the books piled atop them. Ancient spines, cracked and frayed, leaned against one another like tired little soldiers. A Persian carpet runner stretched along the hardwood floor, its edges curling slightly. I stepped around the carpet to avoid the sure plummet I envisioned from my shoes catching the sides.

Behind me, Finn let the door click shut, and the sound echoed too loudly.

"We shouldn't be here," he murmured, shifting uncomfortably.

Ellie ignored him, as seemed to be her plan for the day, her eyes scanning the space. "Where do we start looking?"

"It would help to know what we're searching for," Finn said in a hushed tone.

I glanced down the long hallway grimly. "We should start with anything that has to do with the ship," I said. "It's our main lead."

I nodded toward the study, right beyond the hallway. The French doors were slightly ajar, and I could see Henry's tomes and notebooks strewn all over the wide wood desk in the center.

A draft curled through the house, and I shivered, wrapping my arms around my chest. The motion did little to abate the cold that seeped into my bones and paralyzed my body. Slowly, we marched toward the study, stopping only to glance at the pictures that lined the hallway walls. All of them were newspaper clippings Henry saved over the years and all of them had something to do with the Hollow Siren. I read the heading on one of the clippings that appeared to be from around the same time that the ship first vanished.

Wealthy Couple Vanishes Under Mysterious Circumstances—Friends and Family Baffled; Police Stumped.

My pulse thrummed in my veins. *We're all baffled, aren't we?*

We entered the study, and I ran my fingers along the edge of a table near the entryway, dust clinging to my skin. The house felt abandoned, but not empty. Books lined the walls in here as well, the smell of them clinging to the air. A coat still hung on the rack near the door, as if Henry might walk in at any moment to grab it, complaining about the chill.

But he wouldn't.

We were alone here.

At least, I hoped we were.

There was a loud rumble as a book fell off a nearby shelf. My muscles tensed. Head swinging around, I turned to the far-right wall, only to see Ellie's cheeks redden as she balanced several more books in her grasp. She winced, her eyebrows lowering. "Oops. The man sure liked to read, huh?"

"He *was* a historian," I said. "Did you find anything on that shelf?"

"Nothing new. A lot of books about the Hollow Siren. Shocking, I know. But other than that, there doesn't seem to be anything suspicious." She opened one book, then closed it. Dust swirled around her, rising from inside the pages like a mummy awakened. Ellie coughed into the sleeve of her black sweater. "It would have been nice if Henry spent some time cleaning instead of obsessing over the ship. The place is a mess."

She was right; it truly was quite awful in here. When we first walked in, I assumed the musty aroma was because of how long it had been since someone opened the doors and windows, but I was starting to reconsider that now. I looked around at the balled-up pieces of paper lying around the garbage can in the corner. For lack of a better word, Henry was a bit of a slob. I expected more diligence from the man considering how much attention he paid to details in his work, but perhaps all that energy went elsewhere.

I walked over to the garbage and picked up one of the papers, unfolding it.

"What do you have there?" Ellie asked.

Reading the wrinkled page in my hands, I reached into my purse in search of the gold pen I kept there. After fishing around for a while, I came up empty. Not that it mattered. There was no point writing this information down. It was useless. I balled the paper back up and tossed it in the trash. "Nothing good. Only a receipt for lunch at some place called The Bisque over in King City."

Rolling my gaze over the rest of the study, I opened the small drawer of the side table I stood next to, finding it empty. I wondered why the sheriff sent us here. As far as I could tell, there was nothing here but Henry's research and work materials. Maybe we should check the rest of the house.

"This is strange," Finn said.

He stood by the large desk that took up the majority of the room, his fingers clutching a small bundle. As I approached, I realized it was an emerald green velvet pouch with a ribbon tied around the top. I inched closer to Finn, Ellie sidling in beside me. "Was that in his desk?"

Finn nodded. "Buried under a stack of paperwork and receipts. Looks important."

Slowly, he untied the ribbon and let it flutter down to the desk. Finn turned over the pouch, held out his palm, and shook it to let whatever contents lay inside it to drop out. A clunk sounded in the room as a dull metal pendant tumbled from the pouch and into his open hand. My eyes widened to moons as Finn twirled the pendant around to get a better look. The shine was gone, and the metal corroded, but there was no mistaking it.

I gasped.

"That's Isadora Whitmore's necklace!" I announced. "I'm sure of it. It's the same one she wore the day they took the photo near the ship. The one Henry showed us during his presentation."

Finn poked his head closer to the necklace, the

muscle in his jaw twitching. "I believe you're right. Could it really be the same one?"

"And why does Henry have it hidden in his study?"

Next to me, Ellie scoffed. "Isn't it obvious? He found the treasure! Or at least part of it." She breathed out a low whistle through her teeth. "No way."

"Let's not jump to conclusions. We don't know if it's the same pendant," I said. "It could be a fake."

"I can take it to my appraiser to get a confirmation," Ellie suggested. "But I know this is the same one. He found it! He actually found it!"

I raised an arched brow at her. "You have an appraiser?"

"I have many things," Ellie replied cheekily. She snatched the pendant from Finn, depositing it back in the pouch, and shoving it into her backpack. "I'll go right away. Are you two all right to catch a cab home? This cannot wait!"

Not bothering to hear our reply, she turned around and rushed out of the house, kicking up dust in her dramatic exit. The study was somehow larger without her in it and my lungs expanded to suck in a big breath.

I turned to Finn. "She is really into this."

"That's Ellie for you. Always all in," Finn said. "Come on, I'll call us a cab. I want to get out of here."

Though I didn't say it, I felt much the same way. Being in Henry's house was giving me all sorts of bad feelings, and I couldn't wait to get out and get home. It didn't take very long for the taxi to arrive—a shiny blue car that smelled like lavender and chocolate inside. I rested my head against the window as the car climbed the winding roads alongside the cliffs, taking us further from Henry's home and closer to the manor. As we reached higher altitude, my brain fogged up with thoughts of the necklace and the Whitmores. *What were you doing with that pendant, Henry?* I couldn't wrap my mind around it. Ellie was convinced that the treasure was found, but I didn't agree. If Henry did find the Hollow Hoard, why keep it a secret? The man's entire reputation rested on solving the mystery of the ship, and I would think finding it would be a gargantuan deal. He'd be shouting it from the rooftops, not hiding pendants in his study.

Finn's phone rang, the lively tune filling the cab.

"Hello?" He asked. His face grew ashen, and his brows dropped low over his darkening eyes. A storm brewed in his expression, one that made me press deeper into the cab's leather seat. "We'll meet you there," he said. Then, tapping our driver on the shoulder, added, "Sorry to do this, but we need to go somewhere else. It's an emergency."

"What's going on?" I asked, my voice pitching.

Finn peeled his eyes from the driver to gaze at me. There was a mix of fear and panic in him that I hadn't seen before, and it made me want to jump out of the moving vehicle. I bit down on my bottom lip, hard. "You're scaring me. What happened and where are we going?"

"That was Rosemary," Finn said. "Someone tried to run Ellie off the road. They're on the way to the hospital now."

"Oh no! Is she okay?"

Finn rubbed the bridge of his nose until the skin turned red. "I don't know. Rosemary sounded really scared, so I don't think it's good. We'll know more once we get there."

Our eyes met, an understanding passing between us. With the driver so close, we couldn't say what we wanted to, but both of us knew what this meant. It was no accident that someone tried to hurt Ellie, not with the Whitmore pendant in her grasp. My heart sank to my toes. Someone knew we were in that house and they knew what we found. And I was willing to bet it was the same person who killed Henry. Terror ran its icy fingers down my spine.

We didn't only find a clue to the puzzle today, we also put ourselves on the killer's radar.

Chapter Fifteen

The hospital sat on the edge of town, a wide, three-story brick building with a massive, polished sign out front that read *Holbeck General Hospital*. The parking lot was half-full, mostly with sedans and pickup trucks, and the bright spotlights alongside the front of the building cast long shadows on the concrete as we walked up to the front entrance. The scent of asphalt and faint exhaust lingered in the air, making me pull up the turtleneck of my sweater to avoid inhaling it.

For some reason, I expected Finn's workplace to be posher than the place we arrived at, but what did I know of hospitals? The one in Holbeck that we were at now was the closest to Orchard Hollow and it wasn't like I had much experience getting sick. Fairies couldn't catch a human ailment and if I was ill, it wouldn't be anything my green magic couldn't treat.

The automatic glass doors slid open with a whoosh, and the smell of antiseptic and coffee immediately filled my senses. My nose was sure getting a workout today. Inside, the waiting room was a mix of green and beige, with scuffed linoleum floors and rows of outdated magazines stacked on white metal tables. A few people sat in yellow plastic chairs, some scrolling on their phones, others staring out the large wall-to-wall window on one side of the room. Behind the reception desk, an elderly nurse in pastel pink scrubs was typing something into a computer.

When we approached, she never looked away from her task, only saying, "Take a number at the machine by the bathroom door. I'll call you in a minute."

"Hi, Barbara," Finn said.

The nurse finally peeled her gaze from the screen, a smile tugging at the edges of her lips. "O'Malley! What brings you in? I don't have you on the schedule today," she said. Her hands typed on the keyboard, the clacks echoing through the room. "Nope. Nothing here."

"I'm not on," Finn said. "Not until the weekend. We're here for less than happy news, I'm afraid. A friend was in a car accident, and they brought her here. I was hoping you could tell me which room she's in."

Barbara the nurse did not appear to trust me because her eyes narrowed to slits as she watched me over the tall counter. Finally, she unlocked her gaze, and I was able to take in a breath.

"A friend? What's her name honey? I'll look it up."

Finn smiled warmly. "Ellie Blackwood."

A few more clacks and some groans from Barbara had me in knots. Was Ellie all right? Rosemary had very little information when she called, so it was up to our imagination to come up with the worst-case scenario. Which we did the entire drive into Holbeck. It was a nightmare.

"Third floor. Room 312," Barbara said. A printed visitor's pass slid across the counter. Her eyes pinned me in place. "You have to wear this. Visitors need a pass."

I mumbled a "thank you" under my breath and clipped the pass to my sweater. The metal clip pulled on the yarn, making a gaping hole above my collar bone. *Thanks a million, Barb.*

Next to me, Finn rapped his knuckles on the counter, his back straightening out. "Thanks, Barbara. You're the best."

"Don't you forget it," the nurse replied. "I mean that. My birthday is coming up."

With that, she went back to her previous task, paying us no more mind. I followed Finn down the long corridor to the right and through a set of wide swinging doors until we reached the main elevator.

The ride up was slow, the hum of the machinery filling the silence. When the doors finally opened, the third floor was quieter than the lobby, save for the occasional beep of medical monitors and the murmur of voices from nearby rooms. The hallway had bright white walls that seemed to be freshly scrubbed, much like everything else in the hospital. It was such a juxtaposition to the manor that I couldn't help but shrink a little. Being here in this sterile environment was not the least bit comforting, and I felt sorry for the people who had to spend all their days here. We passed a room with a blue curtain drawn around a hospital bed. I felt even worse for those staying due to medical conditions.

Room 312's door was slightly ajar, the light from inside spilling into the already bright hallway. Stepping in, we were met with the sight of Ellie lying in the hospital bed, a thin blanket draped over her, an IV-line snaking from her arm. The same blue curtain hung behind her. Ellie's face was paler than usual, a bruise blooming across her temple. Standing next to the bed was Rosemary and a woman I didn't recognize sat in an uncomfortable-looking chair behind her. The woman had the same nose and eyes as Rosemary, and I instantly recognized her as Rosemary's mother.

This should be interesting.

We waved sheepishly as we approached the bed. I was relieved to see Ellie's eyes fly open. Now that I was closer, she looked a lot healthier than she did from the doorway and hope fluttered in my chest.

"You look like hell," Finn murmured, sidling up next to Rosemary. He nodded to Rosemary and her mother. "Could have dressed up for the party."

Ellie gave a breathy laugh. "You should see the other guy—well, the tree."

The tension that had gripped my chest loosened just a little. Ellie was here. She was alive. And for now, that was enough.

The only non-Warden in the group sighed loudly, and we all turned to look at Rosemary's mother. The woman flung her granny square shawl over her left shoulder, her body shifting uncomfortably in the chair. She sighed dramatically again, saying nothing.

"What is it, Mom?" Rosemary asked, clearly annoyed. Then, motioning toward her vaguely, said, "This is my mother everyone. Delilah Singh."

The woman, Delilah, smiled faintly. "A pleasure, I'm sure," she drawled. "Unlike this chair."

Rosemary's jaw twitched. I tried not to laugh at their exchange, but it was difficult to contain my emotions. The women reminded so much of my mother and I that it was hard not to giggle. Even the way they seemingly frustrated each other despite obviously caring a lot for one another was spot on for how we used to behave back in Fairy. Watching them was the closest to my mother I felt in a long while and my heart fluttered in my chest because of it. It was shortly replaced by a pang of longing that I had to tamp down, so I didn't start crying. My mother was the only thing about home I actually truly missed.

"Why don't you get us some coffees and stretch out?" Rosemary suggested.

Her mother scoffed but stood up, re-wrapping her shawl again, even though it hadn't shifted from its previous position on her slender shoulders. She nodded at Ellie, asking, "Are they allowing you coffee in this prison?"

Ellie chuckled.

"I'll pay you a million bucks to sneak one in," she said. "Another million if you can round up a cinnamon bun."

With a wink, Delilah pushed past her daughter and headed for the door, an air of self-assurance wafting behind her as she walked.

I started after her. "I'll come with you," I suggested. "It might be a lot to carry. And I could use the bathroom."

We made our way out of the room and back into the hallway. In the distance, alarms wailed, and footsteps echoed through the sterile space as whatever emergencies plagued the hospital took over the evening. I shuffled my feet on the linoleum and the noise they made caused me to wince with every step. Ahead of me, Delilah moved like a woman on a mission, her steps long and quick as she put more and more distance between us. When she reached a fork in the hallway, she gestured to the sign on the wall that pointed to the hospital cafeteria and took off in the direction it suggested. Her back retreated to a small dot before vanishing from my sight entirely.

I glanced around the hallway, finding the sign for the bathroom easily. My bladder was fuller than a well and I sped up, rushing into the closest restroom I could find. I was in such a hurry that I didn't notice the nurse exiting one of the stalls. My head collided with hers with a loud, dull thud, our foreheads knocking together. Searing pain shot through my rattling brain.

I stepped back, rubbing the sore spot. Embarrassment flushed my skin. I opened my mouth to apologize but stopped the second I saw who I ran over.

No Fairy way...

Standing before me and rubbing a twin red spot on her head was none other than the woman I saw Duncan with at The Whistling Kettle. There was no denying it; she was an identical match. I rolled my gaze over the nurse's scrubs she wore, and the small name tag pinned to her shirt. Mila Wren. Obstetrics.

"I'm sorry, I didn't see you there," Mila said. Her voice had a sing-song quality to it that bounced off the mint tiles of the bathroom walls. "One of those days, you know?"

I closed my gaping jaw and worked to wipe the dumbfounded look off my face. Shaking my head, I pulled my hand down from my aching forehead and attempted a friendly smile. "Completely my fault. I should watch where I'm going."

"Trust me, running people over is unavoidable in this place," Mila said. "Well, I'll let you get to it."

She stepped aside to let me through, but I didn't budge. This was it—my chance to find out more about Duncan. I couldn't let this moment slip through my fingers even if it meant cornering the nurse in the bathroom. Despite her friendly demeanor, she was still the same woman who was dating an attached man.

I rolled out my shoulders. "You seem very familiar," I said. "Didn't I see you with Duncan Price on Cliff Row last week?"

The blood drained from the nurse's face, leaving her pale as a sheet. Her body sagged, as if the weight of an invisible force pressed down on it. Her eyes flicked rapidly from side to side, wild with panic, the whites stark against her paling complexion. A tremor ran through her fingers as she clutched at the fabric of her scrubs, her breath coming in short, uneven gasps. She swayed on unsteady legs, teetering backward, her grip fumbling for support that wasn't there.

Hitting the tiled wall, Mila gritted her teeth as she glared at me. "I'm afraid you're mistaken. I don't know anyone by that name."

"Are you sure?" I asked.

"Y-yes. Yes, of course," Mila stuttered. She pushed away from the wall and stumbled toward the exit. "I need to get back to work. Have a good day."

I held up my hand. "Wait!"

But Mila was gone, the door swinging shut behind her. She ran out of the bathroom so fast I was surprised there wasn't a Mila-shaped hole in the wall. What was that about? *She must know that Duncan is with Eloise. Why else would she run?* Except that didn't seem to be the bulk of whatever troubled her. The way Mila reacted was more intense than someone caught in a cheating scandal, and I was willing to bet that there was more to her relationship with Duncan than I realized.

Something about being seen with Duncan spooked the nurse, and I intended to find out what. I glanced at the bathroom stalls, my knees knocking together. Not right now, though.

Step one: pee.

Step two: make sure Ellie is settled in well and feeling great.

Step three: find out what Duncan and Mila were hiding.

I checked off the to do list in my head, my resolve hardening with every passing second. Who knew that a trip to the hospital could be the thing that turned this entire case around?

Chapter Sixteen

"Have you heard from Ellie?" I asked Mortimer.

"She's out of the hospital, but they're having her stick to her bed for a while," the old man replied. "Safe to say she is not too pleased with that."

We sat in the wing-backed chairs in the secret library, our laps warmed by the heat emanating from our respective laptops. The silence in the hidden retreat was a lovely reprieve from the manor, and when Mortimer asked me to join him today, I all but jumped at the invitation. Anything to be away from my racing thoughts and uneasy heart.

A draft rushed by me, swinging my loose waves of hair around my face. I pushed myself up with the arms of the chair to look at the door. It was closed tightly so the draft couldn't have come from there.

I settled back down and looked at Mortimer. "Is there another entrance to this place?"

"Just the one," Mortimer said. Another gust of light wind trotted by us and his pointed nose sharpened. "Oh, the breeze. That happens from time to time. Someone is probably in the mausoleum."

My eyes went saucer round. "I thought no one used it anymore. Isn't it why you all meet here?"

Mortimer shrugged, his attention flitting back to his laptop. "It's a public cemetery. Probably kids playing around up there," he said. "I used to do the same thing when I was young."

The idea that Mortimer was ever anything in his life but an ancient mortician was beyond me. I tried to picture it, I truly did, but the image nearly broke my brain. Instead, I focused on ignoring the slight drafts that continued to flow through the library and unscrewed the carafe of tea I brought in with me, pouring a second cup for both myself and Mortimer.

I took a sip and relished in the deliciousness of the brew—a vanilla orchid blend I picked up last week from Mrs. Dawson. The one thing that I loved most about this realm was the tea. Hands down. Humans were great—when they weren't killing each other for the most ridiculous reasons—but the tea, that was the real magic of

Earth. I licked my lips, setting down the cup on top of the wooden coaster on the side table.

"Have you thought about what happened to Ellie?" I asked Mortimer.

The man's face wrinkled as he took in my words. "The accident?"

I nodded.

"Or the convenience of the timing?" Mortimer added. When I gave another curt nod, he said, "I'd have to be either daft or ignorant not to connect those dots. For someone to run her off the road at the exact moment that she had the necklace on her ... It has to be related."

"But why not take the necklace if that's what they were after?"

Mortimer rubbed the short beard on his chin. "Perhaps they weren't after the necklace. It's possible whoever caused the accident was trying to send a message."

"To Ellie?"

"To all of us. Back off or you're next," Mortimer said grimly. "Besides, the police were on the scene very quickly, so it's also possible they didn't have time to grab the necklace."

A grimace tugged at my lips, pulling them down. It was all very plausible, of course. Everything Mortimer was saying made sense, and yet I didn't understand the most important part about Ellie's accident. I didn't understand *why* someone would want to attempt to hurt her, mortally even, and not try to take the necklace. If we did in fact have Isadora Whitmore's prized possession and with it in hand were close to finding the ship and its treasure, wouldn't it stand to reason that the necklace was worth a fortune? Why not take it?

Unless Mortimer was right, and the police scared the driver of the car off. Who knew at this point?

The mortician grumbled under his breath and stood up from the chair. His back creaked and groaned in protest as his bones readjusted into a new position. Mortimer cracked his spine, the sound making goosebumps spread over my arms and legs.

He shut his laptop, cramming it into the worn-out leather briefcase he carried it in. "I'm afraid I have to leave you for now," Mortimer said. "I have an appointment I can't miss."

"At the funeral home?"

"I'm afraid not. I have to drop by Finn's hospital," Mortimer answered. A darkness crossed his features briefly. "The police would like a statement from me as a character witness for him."

I gulped. "No luck getting him off the hook for the trial yet?"

"Not so far, no," Mortimer said. "We'll keep at it."

"Do you need any help? I'm happy to lend a hand."

And to get my mind off all the other trouble I'm in.

Mortimer waved his hand in the air dramatically. "That's all right, Lyra. You've got your hands full with the case and considering Ellie's situation, I'd say that has to be our priority for now. I only wish I didn't have to run off for this nonsense and leave you to it alone."

"No worries," I said. "I could use some time to myself anyhow. I'll let you know if I find anything."

As Mortimer stalked out of the library and locked the door behind him, I let my gaze travel over the towering bookshelves, my stomach twisting and turning. I probably shouldn't have left Theo alone in the manor, all things considering. The cat was pretty decent at staying out of sight, but I wasn't sure what he would do if Rhyven returned. If only there was some magical way I could protect the manor from the nasty prince. There was no point dwelling on it now. Whatever I could manage to scrape up on the magic side of things, chances were Rhyven would know how to break the spells. He wasn't a royal heir for no reason. Fae kings and queens didn't pass on the crown to just any child; they needed to wield magic that was strong enough to sustain the court, and I was willing to bet that Rhyven had magic up the wazoo.

Teeth clenching, I forced myself to focus on the open website before me and not on any impending doom awaiting me, concentrating on the task at hand. My lips moved as I read out the title of the blog I had pulled up earlier. "The Cursed Hoard," I whispered into the damp air.

Talk about gloomy. I wasn't even sure why the article came up when I was searching for information on Mila Wren, Duncan's local mistress. The woman was a nurse, for Fairy's sake. When I saw the title, I couldn't help but explore further, knowing it must have been about the Hollow Siren. Not many other treasures out there with their own name—the Hollow Hoard had earned itself a reputation over the years with treasure enthusiasts and professional treasure hunters alike.

I looked at the date, noting it down in the small notebook in my lap. The article was published around three years ago. I didn't know if the information would be useful, but it never hurt to jot things down.

My eyes scanned the lit-up screen, stopping only periodically at moments of importance. The majority of the blog post discussed the speculated treasure aboard the Hollow Siren in excruciating detail, going as far as to list all the items of note people said were stashed away over the years. I stopped scrolling when I saw a name that rang a bell.

"Radcliffe ..." I scratched the back of my head. "Why does that seem familiar?"

Flipping through the notebook, I turned the pages until I reached the section on Duncan. It was a short list with very few notes since I found nothing important on the guy. All except one thing: the company he worked for as a treasure hunter.

My legs stretched out long. "Radcliffe Ventures and Expeditions."

Clicking on a new tab, I typed the name into the search bar and pulled up the company's website. According to their information page, Radcliffe Ventures and Expeditions had been in business for over a decade and prided themselves on successful expeditions, specifically those that dealt with discoveries of lost things. I wondered if they were after the Hollow Hoard. It would explain Duncan's presence in town around the time Henry was presenting. He did mention having a professional interest in the historian's work.

Digging further, I found out that the company was founded by Daphne Radcliffe, a well-known adventurer who started the business after a sordid divorce that left her with a hefty sum of money.

I opened a third tab and typed in Daphne's name, pulling up several articles on the woman. As much as I hated to admit it, she was very impressive. Apparently, Daphne was the definition of a boss because the woman had built herself up into the driving force behind some of the most amazing discoveries. From diving off the coast of Fiji to treading in the rainforest, there was not a treasure that Daphne's company was not willing to seek.

A name popped up at me on the screen. My heart

stopped beating for a brief moment before picking up the pace again, doubling my speed. I clicked on the 'Read More' button with a trembling finger. My mouth gaped and the rear of my neck was slick with sweat.

"This can't be real."

Except it was. I checked three more sources, and they all confirmed what I saw on the first page. Daphne Radcliffe was Mila's stepmother.

I bit down on my tongue, the taste of iron filling my mouth. "That's the connection!"

By the time I finished spiraling down the rabbit hole of the internet, my tea was ice cold, and my toes lost all blood flow from sitting in the same position. There was nothing else of real value to add to what I already found, but that didn't matter. What I had was enough. Mila, Duncan, and now Radcliffe Ventures and Expeditions. It was all connected to Henry somehow. I knew it. Checking the time, I decided it was time to crawl out of my hiding spot and return home; I would tell the Wardens about this later. I closed the million tabs I had opened one by one, my laptop feeling lighter by the second. I was about to close down the last one when another passage pulled at me.

I pressed my nose closer to the screen, my eyes growing in size.

"I got it!"

Chapter Seventeen

It was official. I had managed to anger the cat enough not to speak to me. Apparently, being gone for half the morning was the thing that pushed Theo over the edge, and he spent the remainder of the day giving me the cold shoulder and taking over the clawfoot tub to use as his personal snack-eating fortress. Which was completely fine by me since I had made plans anyhow.

The type of plans that required me slinking off after the sun went down to meet a woman about a treasure hunt. Well, a fake treasure hunt.

That's right! Daphne Radcliffe agreed to meet me to discuss the expedition I wanted to hire her company to pursue. It was all a load of fairy mush, but Daphne didn't know that. What was I going to do when she figured it out? I had no idea. For now, I was glad to have a chance to find out what happened between Henry and her all those years ago. According to my sleuthing, the two had a massive falling out that ended with both attacking one another on every social media forum popular in the treasure hunting community. Most of the posts had been removed due to unbecoming language, but I was able to deduce that they had something to do with the Hollow Siren, specifically Daphne's interest in the ship.

With that information in tow and Theo's incredulous looks as he passed by me while I was cramming my boots on, I was off on the forty-five-minute drive to King City. Outside the truck window, the world darkened, and the sun dipped below the horizon; the scenery zooming by in a swirl of reds and oranges. I focused my eyes on the road as I left the vastness of our small-town roads and entered the more densely populated city. All around me, people rushed from one destination to another, some even jumping in front of my very slow-moving vehicle to jaywalk across the street.

My heart raced in my chest, my foot jerking from the gas to the brakes.

By the time I parked outside of a tall, glass-encased building, I was covered in nervous sweat and breathing like I had run a marathon. I climbed out of the truck on shaky legs and made my way to the revolving doors in front of me. The sign for Radcliffe Ventures and Expeditions flashed in a neon red above the entrance with a large X marking the doors. It was a clever nod to pirate-life. I wondered if Daphne would appreciate my thinking of her as a modern-day pirate or if she'd scorn me for the reference.

I pushed through the doors and into the belly of the modern, minimalist building. Air whooshed behind me as the doors continued their rotation, finally stopping a few moments later. The lobby of the office was as exciting as the inside of a portal. That is to say that it was mostly empty and smelled a little damp. I brushed my hand over the leaf of a large Ficus plant and recoiled when I realized it was fake. Now that I had the chance to look around, fake was a word I would use for most of the decor in the lobby. The frames displaying various expeditions were shiny faux plastic made to resemble wood molding. The leather of the seats smelled of turpentine and plastic. Even the carpet under my feet felt like it was made from unnatural fibers.

For all intents and purposes, Daphne's office had all the surface frills, with none of the luxury.

I didn't know why, but I had the feeling most places in the city had a similar air of false grandeur.

"Lyra Moore?"

I spun around to a narrow doorway on the far side of the lobby where a tall, slim woman with four-inch heels and a pencil skirt tighter than my medical gloves stood with expectant eyes. Her chocolate brown hair was peppered in perfectly positioned grays, and she had skin so smooth I never would have given her more than thirty years, though according to her online profiles she was well in her sixties. Everything about the woman was immaculate, down to the shapely eyebrow she crooked at me when I still hadn't answered.

I cleared my throat, spurred to action. "Hi, yes. That's me," I mumbled. "Are you Daphne Radcliffe?"

The woman extended a sculpted arm. I took her hand, giving it a light shake despite her grip being that of a hungry shark.

"One and the same. Thanks for coming by," Daphne said. "Would you like a coffee?"

I looked at the fake-gold clock on the wall. Six in the evening. Shaking my head, I said, "I'm okay. And thank you for seeing me on such short notice."

Daphne nodded, pointing to the doorway where she stood, which I took as a sign to follow her in. Once inside, she pulled out a metal chair for me and skirted around a glass desk to sit down. The desk, like the rest of the office, was almost entirely clear of clutter. Aside from the sleek laptop the color of a shell, Daphne had nothing on her desk save for a designer agenda and a pen holder. The pen holder had a dozen of the same gold pens inside it, each one completely unused and clearly only there for decoration.

I slipped into the chair, my bones protesting the discomfort of it instantly.

"Tell me about the project," Daphne said, getting straight to business. "You mentioned a yacht that went down?"

My brain cells rubbed together as I tried to recall exactly what web of lies I had told the woman to earn a meeting tonight. Peeling my lips back from my teeth, I forced a meek smile, saying, "My great-grandfather's yacht, yes. The family has been searching for years with no success."

"Interesting," Daphne mused. She typed a few words into the laptop. "Do you have copies of the notes on the previous attempts? Maps are good too, but I understand if you don't have those in your possession."

"I can see what I can dig up," I lied.

Daphne gave me a curt nod. "That's good. It's a start," she said. "Has your family hired other discovery companies or was it all personally handled?"

"You're the first one we turned to."

Her green eyes flicked up from the screen to glance at me. "Interesting. Who is funding the project?"

Needles spread down my thighs. I really should have spent more time perfecting my cover story on the drive over instead of daydreaming. Of course,

Daphne needed to know the details! As far as she was concerned, I was about to hand her a gargantuan amount of money to go gallivanting in search of this made-up yacht. She wouldn't start a project without having all the information up front. From what I'd read about the woman—treasure hunting and the stigma that went along with it aside—she was a true professional. And very highly respected in her field.

I crossed my legs, the needles spreading down to my toes.

"My father will be funding it," I told Daphne finally.

She took a few more notes before asking, "And how did you hear about Radcliffe?"

"Actually," I started, jumping at the chance to get to the real purpose of the visit. "I saw that you worked on a similar project. The Hollow Siren, I believe."

Daphne's fingers hovered over the keyboard of her laptop. Her jaw ticked, and she snapped it shut, lowering her hands to rest rigidly on the tabletop. "If you're here because of that expedition, I have to warn you, we didn't recover the ship," she said. "The project was a complete disaster from the start."

"Oh? How so?"

Daphne cringed visibly. "I'm not sure how much you know about the stories surrounding the ship and its voyage, but the contradicting information made it nearly impossible to follow the trail."

"I could see how that would make it hard to work on," I agreed. I folded my arms over my chest. "Come to think of it, my friend said the very same thing when he talked about the ship. He was quite the history buff and was very interested in the Siren too."

"Your friend?" Daphne asked.

I met her questioning gaze with a serious glare. "Henry Barlow."

At this, her fingers curled into tight fists, the knuckles turning to a pasty white from the force of her grip. She gritted her teeth, the sound carrying through the room like nails on a chalkboard. Daphne's eyes never left mine when she shut her laptop with a hollow thud.

"I'm afraid I can't help you, Miss Moore," she said curtly.

I slanted my brows. "Why not?"

"I made a personal promise not to get involved with anything Barlow touched again," she replied. "I'm afraid that promise extends to his friends. The man was unbearable and had cost me a lot of money, not to mention time and patience."

"That's a shame. Henry never mentioned anything," I said. "What happened between you two? I can't imagine Henry having a disagreement with anyone, if I'm being honest."

Daphne guffawed. "Well, perhaps you didn't have the pleasure of being on his bad side then," she said. She was so worked up I could almost see steam pouring from her flaring nostrils. "A word of advice, Miss Moore. Don't trust the man's word if he tries to help you with your mission. Henry Barlow will say anything to prove his point, whether his words are factual, or not."

"That doesn't sound like the Henry I knew."

"Well, it sure sounds like the one I did," Daphne rebutted. "Did you know we started working on the search for the Siren together? As a team?" When I shook my head, she scoffed. "Of course, he wouldn't share that part. Henry came to me for help ages ago, claiming he knew where to find the ship and that, given the right partnership, he could finally solve the mystery hounding the world for decades. It was all fairy tales in the end. The man had nothing but dreams and guesses and when I told him to abandon ship, no pun intended, he decided he'd rather drag my name through the mud than listen to reason."

My body froze. "I can't believe he'd do that."

"Believe it," Daphne said angrily. "Henry is obsessed with the ship, and nothing can sway him from it. I wouldn't be surprised if he'd keep searching, even if someone told him the ship never existed in the first place. He's not the first historian to be interested in the ship, but he's certainly the most passionate."

"You've worked with others who had the same interest?"

Daphne shook her head. "Not worked but crossed paths with. There was one in particular that I seem to recall, someone Henry mentioned. Knowing Henry, he probably tried to ruin that poor sap as well. The man did not handle competition well, as you can probably guess from our history."

She stood up, sauntering toward the office door and beckoning me to follow. As we walked back to the lobby, Daphne glanced back, throwing a last remark over her shoulder. "Take my advice, Lyra," she said. "Avoid Henry Barlow like the plague. And don't give him any money."

Daphne waited until I piled myself into the revolving doors and left to lock up the office. Her eyes followed me the entire time I marched back to the truck, following me still as I clawed my way into the driver's seat. When she finally turned around and left, I breathed out. I glared at my reflection in the rear view. The muscles in my arms twitched.

The entire time Daphne Radcliffe spoke about Henry, she used the present tense. I swallowed the hot lump in my throat.

She didn't know he was dead.

With that nugget of knowledge tucked into the back of my mind, I turned on the ignition and started the long drive home. At this time of the night, the streets of King City were even tougher to cut through than they were coming in with people crowding the sidewalks and zigzagging across the road to get to their destination. Luckily, Orchard Hollow was as sleepy as ever and I found myself able to breathe steadily again when the city was far behind me and the calmness of our small town took over.

I maneuvered the truck up the winding road on the cliffs, parking it in the driveway in the pitch black of the cool evening.

The manor was darker than the cavernous streets of the Shadow Court and the glimmer of moonlight that streamed in through the windows cast ominous shadows over the hardwood, making the place appear more eerie than it should. I flicked on the lights as I strolled through the house. There was no need to make a funeral home even creepier, not with all the dead bodies in the basement.

"Theo!" I yelled out.

A second later, a hoarse moan alerted me from the living room. My senses jumped to attention immediately. *What did that cat get into now?*

I rushed down the main hallway, skidding to a stop in front of the living room doors. From here, the scene before me was straight out of a gothic novel. Theo lay sprawled on the couch, his furry head propped up on a pillow and his legs drooping to the side. His eyes were half shut, and he appeared to be attempting to focus them when he spotted me in the doorway. My heart leaped into my throat.

Running to the changeling, I kneeled beside him, asking, "Theo? What happened?"

He opened his mouth, but no sound came out, only another hoarse moan followed by his eyes fluttering and rolling into the back of his head. I screamed.

"No! No, no, no!"

Hovering over Theo, I pressed my cheek to his nose, relieved to feel the breath expel from his lungs. His breathing was labored and slow, but at least it was there. My eyes scanned the living room to see what might have happened, but I didn't spot anything out of place. Theo gasped. I looked at him, fear swallowing me whole. From the looks of the cat, it seemed that time was not on our side.

Tears flowed down my cheeks and all the way to my neck. I pressed my palms to Theo's chest, feeling it rise and fall under my skin. Panic shot through me and with it, my magic coiled over my arms and chest, enveloping both the cat and me in a rainbow sparkle. Under my touch, the cat inhaled a sharp breath, then another.

Keeping one hand on his chest, I reached for my phone and dialed the town vet's number that I had saved to my contacts after the last time Theo got into the gardening shed and scratched his leg on a rusty nail.

The line rang several times before a friendly woman picked up on the other side. "Orchard Hollow Veterinary Clinic. How can I help you today?"

"My cat," I breathed out. "Something is wrong with my cat. He passed out and I can't get him to wake up. And his breathing is all off. It seems better now, but he's still not awake."

"Stay calm, miss," the woman instructed. "Do you think you can move him? We can get you in immediately."

I looked at Theo. What choice did I have? Bundling him close to my chest, I squeezed the phone between my ear and shoulder and bolted to the front door. "I'll be there in fifteen minutes," I told the woman on the line.

After securing Theo on the floor of the passenger side atop a blanket I kept in the truck, I climbed into the vehicle and started it up. My attention zapped to the phone on the seat. I grabbed it rapidly, sending out a fast text to Finn to meet me at the vet, then took off. I wasn't sure if he would get it or if he would be able to come, but I knew that I didn't want to be alone right now. And strangely, Finn was the first person I thought to reach out to.

Chapter Eighteen

We sat in the cold waiting room of the vet's office in silence. I stared blankly at the mural of animals in hats on the opposite wall of the room, my hands folded lamely in my lap. Beside me, Finn shifted his weight uncomfortably, but didn't utter a word. It was nice to be quiet together while we waited for the vet to return with news on Theo. They had taken him to be examined a while ago and we still had no answers.

I checked the clock on the wall, my blood pressure spiking. "What's taking so long?"

"He's in good hands," was all Finn said. "He will be fine."

Somehow, I wasn't so sure.

I looked around the space we occupied and frowned.

The waiting room was too bright, too sterile, the sharp scent of antiseptic and wet animal lingering in the air. The other walls were painted a pastel blue, probably meant to be calming, but it only made the room feel colder. Although that could have been my dark mood cooling down my tired bones. I pulled my sweater tighter around me, but it didn't help. Nothing would, not until I knew if Theo would be all right.

Finn hunched forward, his elbows on his knees, fingers laced together so tightly his knuckles had gone pale. His foot tapped against the linoleum in an uneven rhythm, stopping only when the door to the main exam rooms swung open. Every time, my heart lurched, only for a tech or a vet to call someone else's name. Not ours.

What was taking so long?

I pressed my hands together in my lap, squeezing them until my fingers ached. Somehow, I knew that nasty fae prince had something to do with what happened to Theo. How else could we explain his sudden illness? I never should have left him alone. What was I thinking doing that after the message from Rhyven?

If there was a hell for fairies, I'd burn in it for all eternity.

I kept replaying the moment over and over in my

head: the way Theo had gone limp in my arms, the rush to get him here, the doors swinging shut as the technician took him from me. No matter how much we bickered, Theo was my only true friend in this realm. Family, really. He was the only one who knew who I truly was, and, for all his nonsense, he was a real solid character. I could always count on him in a bind. He just couldn't count on me.

I seriously hated myself.

The clock on the wall ticked forward, indifferent to the fact that every passing second felt like I was running out of air. The tea Finn had stepped out to get sat untouched beside him, the lid still sealed. There was no way I could stomach anything right now.

The door opened again. A vet tech stepped into the waiting room, glancing down at the chart in his hands before looking up.

"Miss Carter?"

My shoulders slumped as I visibly deflated. A woman in her late sixties stood up and followed the tech into the Corridor of Doom. Her relieved laugh echoed toward us and my mood slightly improved, knowing that at least someone else's pet was doing fine. I chewed on my bottom lip until I tasted blood.

"Hey, tell me more about Daphne Radcliffe," Finn said suddenly.

I shook out my hair and ran my fingers through the

limp tresses. "She didn't do it," I said. "Henry and she didn't see eye to eye, but from what I gathered, she didn't care much for the ship or finding it. Actually, she seemed quite nice. Until I mentioned Henry."

"I still can't believe you drove all the way out there on your own. Ask me next time. It could have been dangerous."

"It was only an office building."

Creases marked the sides of Finn's mouth as it turned down. He kept his gaze on the same wall I'd studied earlier, but I could see his eyes dart my way from time to time. He let out an exasperated sigh. "Humor me," he said, his tone serious. "I could have used a drive myself."

The court hearing. Of course! In all my running around and now this disaster with Theo, I had completely forgotten to ask him about it. No wonder he seemed on edge when he met me at the vet tonight; the man must be walking on eggshells with his fate up in the air like that.

I peeled my clammy hand from my lap, wiped it, and placed it on Finn's arm. "No news from the police yet?"

"Not a peep. I'm starting to think they have a thing for me," Finn admitted. "The station is dodging my calls and I've been racking my brain for a way out of this, but nothing comes to mind. I wish there was a loophole of some sort."

"There might be," I said. "Once we find out what's happened to Theo, I'll take a look too. You officially have my services as a sleuth at your disposal."

Finn smiled, and it made the room a little warmer.

"Thanks, Lyra," he said. "I'll take all the help I can get. We can't afford to put a spotlight on our group, not when we're helping others. If only the cops forcing me out into the open knew how much we help the police."

Screws tightened in my head as the vague scent of an idea formed. I licked my bottom lip, pulling on the idea so I could grasp it more fully. Perhaps the police were the answer to Finn's problem, and he didn't even realize it. Sure, the cops putting him on the stand might not be useful, but I had the inkling that I knew someone on the force who might have the power to pull some strings.

I looked at Finn, my eyes twinkling. "We should talk to Romero."

"The Orchard Hollow sheriff?" Finn asked. "What could he do? The case I'm on the line for was in King City."

"This is not information most people know," I explained. "But Romero was a big time Federal Bureau agent before he moved to our town. We're talking way up in the chain. I'm willing to bet he'd be able to pull some strings. And he's a fan of our group, so I'm certain he'll want to help."

The plan earned me another bright smile that made my heart melt.

"That's not a bad idea," Finn said. "Definitely worth a shot."

He opened his mouth to say something else but was interrupted by the door opening again, the same vet tech that emerged before stepping out. He looked at his chart, then scanned the waiting room, his gaze landing on me. My entire body stopped functioning.

"Lyra Moore?" the vet tech asked.

I leaped to my feet and rushed toward him like I was running a sprint. Behind me, Finn grabbed the abandoned teacup and jogged up to join us at the open doors. He handed it to me, and I took it for the simple need to have something to do with my hands.

How does he know me so well already?

I rubbed my forehead, facing the tech. "How is he?"

"Theo is stable. It took us a while to figure out what happened. I apologize for making you wait so long."

"What did happen?" Finn asked before I could.

The vet tech's brow creased, and he glanced at his chart once more, his features grim. "To be honest, I've never seen anything like it," he said. "Your cat most definitely ingested a poison of some kind. It was enough to send his system into shock."

"How is that odd? He may have gotten into something while Lyra was away."

"It's possible," the tech confirmed. "The strange part was that there was no trace of the poison anywhere in his system. Other than the residual way his body was reacting, Theo is as healthy as ever. It was almost as if whatever got to him vanished."

My head spun as I tried to make sense of the explanation. I thought back to finding Theo and the way he was—the vet was right. It definitely looked like he was on his deathbed. But then he seemed to recover quite quickly on the ride over. Right after I ...

I bristled.

It couldn't.

I couldn't have healed him ... could I?

The thought of me suddenly developing healing magic was so preposterous I wanted to laugh. Fairies were a walking magical vault. Everyone had one magic and one magic only. It was their strength and their connection to our realm. My ability to open portals was already a freak accident and now this. No way. I was not willing to entertain the thought. At least, not yet.

I gritted my teeth and concentrated on the matter at hand.

"When can I take him home?" I asked the tech.

The young man smiled. "Give us another hour to double check his vitals, but I'd say you'll be good to go home after that. Theo is very lucky to have you. It was quick thinking getting him down here so fast. Most people go into shock."

"Most people don't surround themselves with dead bodies," I mumbled. When I saw the vet tech's confused expression, I coughed into my hand, saying, "Never mind. Do I need to fill out any paperwork?"

The tech pulled a file folder from his clipboard and handed it to me. "Fill out everything I've highlighted and sign at the bottom of page nine."

I peered into the folder, my attention locking on the letter and number combination at the top of every page. CT204.

"What's that?" I asked the tech.

He shrugged. "Only our internal filing system. C for cat, T for Theo, and the number is the first three of your phone number," he said. "We should really update everything to be online, but after so many years, it would take ages. It's easier to sort through the files at this point."

Leaving me with the folder, he called the next name and brushed past us to greet another pet owner in the waiting room. As the tech walked away, I found myself stuck on the numbers in Theo's file. Finn must have caught me staring because he asked, "What's the matter?"

I shook my head, a laugh bubbling out of me. "I think I know what the cipher for Henry's notebook is."

Chapter Nineteen

Numbers swam in my sightline and blurred together as I continued to decipher Henry's neat writing. Finn and I sprawled on the floor of the Mistbrook Manor library with loose papers and the notebook between us. We split up the deciphering into two parts, with one of us handling reading out the numbered sequence in the notebook while the other jotted down the correct letters in the right place. So far, we'd been able to decode three pages in the notebook, which was not even a fraction of the full thing. Henry was not short onwords, that was certain.

I tapped the pen on my knee while waiting for Finn to read out the next sequence. When he did, I referenced the cipher and jotted down the translation.

"Coroner Street West," I said aloud.

Finn leaned over, cocking his head to read the rest of the passage we translated. "Over by the old factory?" he asked. "Why would Henry have that noted in here?"

I shrugged. Truthfully, I didn't know what Henry was up to anymore.

"Pretty fantastic that he basically told you what the cipher was," Finn added.

"Fantastic is one word for it."

I thought back to the last time the historian visited the manor. *All our time is numbered, a mirror of what we have left on this plane.* That was what Henry said before he left. At the time, I thought he was being his oddball self, but now I knew better; Henry was giving me the cipher code, and I was too blind to see it. The time part was in reference to the watch he left behind; the same one he said he'd like to be buried with if his time should come. I pulled out the watch that I dragged out from storage and looked at the frozen hands behind the glass. Three forty-seven. On the back of the watch, the inscription I thought was that of a family member's name glared at me as I turned the watch over. If we reversed the numbers to seven four three to mirror them, as Henry himself suggested, and assign those to the letters on the back, it gave us the correct cipher code. A was seven, G was four, and T was three. From here, we were able to crack the remainder of the alphabet by applying it to words in Henry's notebook.

It was a pain, but I had to admit, also very exhilarating. I could see why people enjoyed solving riddles or playing those horrifying escape games. The thrill of our discovery was a huge confidence boost. As was getting closer to finding Henry's secrets when it came to the mysterious Hollow Siren.

"What do you think is on Coroner Street?"

I shrugged. "Let's see what the next passage says."

We deciphered several more paragraphs, my head spinning from the continuous strain on my brain to move letters around. The fact that Henry was able to fill an entire notebook with coded writing made him a genius in my book. Or a madman; there were two sides to this coin.

After finishing the passage, we put the translated paper between us and sucked in a communal sharp breath. I narrowed my eyes at the words. "Here lies the truth of the Hollow Siren," I read aloud.

The sentence was followed by a string of numbers that Finn quickly pointed out were likely location coordinates. We pulled them up on a map on his phone, narrowing down the location to a specific spot on Coroner Street.

"Care for a drive?" Finn asked.

I jumped up before he finished speaking. "Let's go! I'm dying to find out what's there." I winced. "Sorry. Terrible choice of words."

"We *are* in a funeral home," Finn teased.

Chuckling, I waited until he got up to skip to the front door with more glee than a fairy in a garden. On the way out, I stopped by the living room where I had set Theo up after we brought him home from the vet. The cat was back to his usual snarky self but had spent the last few hours snoring away to the sound of the television blaring old movie reruns.

I knelt on the floor next to the couch, my face close to Theo's.

"I'm stepping out for a very short while," I whispered to the sleeping changeling. "I promise I'll be back soon. Don't eat anything poisonous."

One amber eye opened to look at me. "Bring back whipped cream."

I laughed.

"I see you're back to your usual self," I said. "Rest up, please. I mean it." Checking to make sure Finn was not in the room, I dragged over the funeral home's landline phone and put it on the coffee table. "If something happens or if someone shows up, call me immediately."

The cat scoffed, closing his eye again. "Stop fussing. If the Shadow Prince shows up, I'll simply dazzle him with my winning personality."

"That's exactly what I'm afraid of."

Theo grumbled a few choice words under his breath before ordering me out of the room. I obeyed without a second word. I really wanted to put the entire fiasco with the ship to rest so I could get back to my life and following the clues Henry left was the key to do so. I just knew it.

Coroner street was a dusty lane smack dab in the center of a dustier abandoned neighborhood on the outskirts of town. Decades ago, there was a fabric factory located here, and a few homes built by those who worked in it. Now that the factory closed, the homes sat abandoned on the depressing street, a constant reminder of a more robust time in Orchard Hollow history.

I marched past an overgrown front yard that reminded me of some of the lusher jungles back in Fairy. My heart skipped a beat at the memory of myself as a child climbing those sky-high trees and leaping off the top to glide down as my small wings flapped madly. Tears stung beneath my eyelids, and I blinked them away, my eyes hot and burning.

"It should be right around here," Finn said, pulling me back from my thoughts.

He pointed to one of the abandoned homes nestled between a tall pine tree and a lot full of broken bricks and scrap metal. A smell hung in the air that reminded me of an oil spill, and I plugged my nose, following Finn to the front porch of the house. Or what used to be a front porch. The wood that wrapped around the front of the decrepit structure was splintered and tinted in a deep green moss that slipped under my feet as I stepped on it to climb up. There were no stairs to help us up, so we had to use each other for balance to scale the dreadful platform.

As we approached the door, painted a lovely shade of vomit brown, I kept my eyes peeled for rusty nails and other items that threatened impalement.

"What could Henry possibly be keeping here?" I asked.

"Not the ship, I wager," Finn replied.

He reached for the handle, stopping his hand an inch above it. Finn reached into his jacket pocket and pulled out a pair of gloves, putting one on and handing one to me. "Just in case," he said.

I nodded, slipping my hand into the glove. I tried not to think that Finn's hand was inside the same glove before.

In one flick of the wrist, Finn twisted the handle and

pushed the door with his shoulder to open it. The wood creaked and groaned as his weight forced our entry, a blast of stale air penetrating our nostrils from inside the house. I coughed into Finn's glove, my eyes watering.

"Let's get through this fast," Finn said.

I nodded, agreeing wholeheartedly. Lost treasure or not, the thought of spending more time here gave me the heebie-jeebies.

The interior of the house was in slightly better shape than the outside and I find I didn't have to hold my breath as the oily smell from outdoors did not penetrate the walls. I spotted a few holes large enough to fit rodents in the walls and frowned. The place was seriously grotesque.

We made a sharp right turn down a dark, menacing corridor and checked every room for anything that might offer some clues as to why we were here. Henry's instructions were vague and gave little away, forcing us to march blindly through the broken-down house in search of ... well, something.

At the end of the corridor, another door greeted us, this one with a small carving on the wood beside the handle. It appeared to be hastily carved into the door with a careful hand. I leaned down to inspect it, my mouth drying.

"It's a ship," I said breathlessly. "This must be it."

We exchanged excited glances before shoving the

door open and bursting inside. My feet skidded to a stop before a large work bench with several industrial machines sitting atop it. The machines were new and shiny and in complete contrast to the rest of the house. I looked at Finn over my shoulder, his somber expression mirroring my own. Slowly, we approached the bench.

The silence in the room was harrowing. A lump formed in my throat and my veins throbbed as blood rushed through them. My eyes doubled in size, taking in the items on the bench.

A row of high-resolution 3D printers sat beside each other, their lenses glimmering in the low light of the room. Next to them, a computer whirred to life when I touched the keyboard on the tabletop. On the screen, side-by-side scans of jewels and coins lit up with an artificial glow. I gulped down air as I inspected the screen, my gaze flicking from the computer to the printers.

I clicked the keyboard again to scroll to a folder on the desktop and pulled it up. Before me, an image of Isadora's necklace took up the screen. Its details were an exact match to the one we found in Henry's study.

Tearing myself away from the computer, I picked up the only other item on the workbench—a notebook that was almost identical to Henry's. I flipped through the pages, which were almost all blank except one. On it, a single sentence made my stomach drop.

"It's not real," I read aloud. Then, turning to Finn, asked, "What does it mean?"

He held up a printout he found in the singular file cabinet in the room while I was snooping at the workbench. The color drained from his face as he said, "This might explain it."

With trembling hands, I took the paper from him. My lips muttered under my breath as I read half out loud and half to myself. The printout was a copy of a ship's mission ledger, one that appeared to be ancient. On it, a list of items took up the majority of the page. Most were of food and supplies, with a few other items that seemed to all coincide with things one might bring on a ship for a long journey.

"What's this?" I asked.

Finn pointed to a passage below the list.

"The contents recovered aboard the Hollow Siren, sunk north of Western Sahara," I read. "Alongside the trunks, the team also exhumed the bodies of Percival Whitmore, Clarence Whitmore, Isadora Whitmore, Henrietta Whitmore, and an unnamed woman of twenty years of age. The bodies will be returned to the family's estate in England on short notice."

"Looks like the treasure was never on the ship," Finn said. "There was never any treasure at all."

I shivered, looking at the machines before me. That wasn't even the worst part, was it? Henry was desperate to make people believe in the Hollow Siren, and it seemed he was willing to do whatever it took to convince people. Even fake a treasure.

Horror laced around my spine. Henry may have known the treasure was fake, but surely he kept that to himself. I shivered.

Henry's own lies got him killed.

Chapter Twenty

And so, it appeared I wasted a lot of precious time chasing clues that led nowhere. To make matters worse, the man whose murderer I was trying to bring to justice was a liar. And a con man, as the evidence would have it. I couldn't believe that Henry would go so far as to fake a treasure. Why? What did he stand to gain? Surely someone would debunk his false jewels and gold, and then what would happen? It didn't make sense to me that someone who had spent half of his life researching the Hollow Siren would risk it all so easily. Henry's entire reputation was on the line, and he was willing to throw it all away over ... what? Plastic necklaces?

No matter how I spun it, the pieces didn't fit.

"Your large head is blocking the television," Theo drawled.

I moved out of the way, putting down the duster I had held and done nothing with for the better part of the hour. My gaze rolled over Theo's reclining form and the crumbs of toast dusting his gray fur. On the bright side, the cat was back to his usual cheerful self again.

Rolling my eyes, I left him to his sitcoms and went to the kitchen where a second pot of tea called my name. The kettle hissed with steam, the smell of lavender filling the room. I inhaled it greedily and poured a tall mug of the delicious concoction. Then, for the first time in a long while, I held my palm over the mug and sprinkled some of my fairy magic into the tea. I was not one for magically infused drinks, especially when my abilities were not to be trusted lately, but your girl needed a boost today. The magical type of boost.

I took a sip of the tea and waited for it to take effect. It only took a few seconds for my muscles to relax and the pounding headache careening between my temples to dissipate. I stared at the mug in my hands. *Wow! I'm getting better at this.*

With my body getting back to normal and my mind no longer racing with random thoughts, I sat down at the kitchen table and pulled Henry's journals toward me. I'd ended up dragging the one we found at the house of lies home with me, setting it aside with the journal

Henry gave me before. As I originally thought, the two were identical. I wondered why the historian kept a second journal hidden away in his lair of deceit—especially since this one was almost entirely blank.

The shroud of mystery surrounding Henry's death was now overshadowed by the one surrounding his life. Perhaps the Henry I knew was not the real him. It was quite possible that beneath the bizarre tales from history and quirky sense of humor, Henry was nothing more than a common criminal. Someone willing to lie to get what he wanted.

I grimaced. I really did not want to believe that.

"I'm running low on toast chips!" Theo yelled from the living room.

My grimace turned into a downright glower. "I'm not your maid!"

"I am recovering, Lyra!" Theo argued. "From a poisoning caused by your inability to marry like a proper royal fae. The least you can do is refill my snack bowl."

He yowled, and the sound made my skin crawl. Leave it to the changeling to cover me in guilt from head to toe. Pushing up from the table, I walked to the butcher block that already had slices of toast from Theo's previous helping on it and sliced them into smaller strips. Then I sprinkled a dash of salt on them —out of spite because the cat hated it—and turned on the oven. While I waited for it to warm, I picked up the two notebooks, holding them up next to each other.

"Why did you give this to me?" I asked the empty kitchen.

I flipped through the pages aimlessly, but no new ideas came to mind. Whatever Henry's reason to lead me to his wicked plan had been, it died with him. All I had now was a blank book and a whole lot of doubt about his character.

The oven beeped, making me jump. I put the notebooks down and opened the door to put the tray of toast in. Steam billowed out from inside and a blast of heat shot into my face. I blinked my wet eyes to clear the fog from my vision. Out of the corner of my eye, the blank page of the second notebook darkened in several spots. The smell of lemon pierced my nostrils.

I blinked rapidly, staring.

There's not a chance.

I picked up the notebook and brought it up to my nose, taking in a long, sharp whiff. I was right.

"Lemons!"

If that the book belonged to anyone else, I never would have considered it, but this was Henry we were talking about, and the man loved his drama. I thought back to the machine in the abandoned house on Coroner Street. Clearly, he was a fan of theatrics. The smell of lemons and the way the pages reacted to the heat from the oven made me instantly think of the story Henry told me when he last visited the funeral home. The one about people using invisible ink to communicate during the war. What were the chances that the lemon I smelled was because Henry had written in the book with it?

Only one way to find out. I put the notebook on the counter and turned on one of the burners.

As soon as I held the book close to the flame, words began to appear on the paper. They were faint, the lemon applied to the page long ago, but they were still there. And the more heat I applied—careful not to burn the manor down, of course—the deeper the shade of brown the letters took on. After twenty minutes of working the flames, I was slick with sweat and had two pages of invisible ink ready to read.

Abandoning Theo's snack, I threw the notebook back on the kitchen table and slid into the chair, my body hunched over it like I was protecting it from the world. In a way, I supposed I was. I needed to keep the heat on the pages as long as possible so I could read what they said. My eyes scanned the words in a rush, and I crammed them into my memory bank as I read the first page, then the next.

There were the same type of entries on both sides.

The notebook appeared to be a log of someone's whereabouts, detailed accounts of a person's comings and goings. The sentences were short and conservative in their description, which I assumed was to save on the lemon juice. There were also dates noted next to each one. Sometimes the entries were several days apart and sometimes there were two or three per day. Those were marked with time stamps next to the dates. The entries bordered on the obsessive and though the ones on the pages I uncovered only spanned one month, I was willing to wager that the remainder of the notebook covered a longer time span.

Who was Henry following, and why?

"The toast!" Theo's voice rattled my brain.

I growled deep in my chest. "It's not ready yet!"

The cat mumbled something that was probably a long strain of cursing. I ignored him, bringing the notebook back to the stovetop so I could unearth the next two pages. This time I was bolder and let the flames rise higher, making the work faster and more efficient. I also read the words as they appeared, which meant that I was continuously sweating through my clothes and hovering over the fire but also getting through more pages.

It was as I thought: the same entries on every single page of each book.

Suddenly, one entry caught my attention. I brought the page closer to the stovetop, my eyes growing in size as I read it. My throat was dry and full, and my tongue swelled in my desert-like mouth, sticking to the sides and not fitting properly between my teeth. I rolled my shoulders and brought the book even closer to the fire, desperate to see if what I thought I read was true.

A spark caught the edge of the paper. Before I could rip the notebook away, flames licked at the lemon-stained pages, setting the entire thing on fire. I shrieked.

Moving with incredible speed, I threw the notebook into the sink and reached for the faucet. My fingers clumsily slid across the metal as the flames inside the sink rose higher and higher. Over my head, the smoke from the fire reached the fire alarm and a blaring louder than a fairy party sounded through the manor. Beyond it, Theo screamed, the sound of his voice getting lost in the incessant blaring.

I finally managed to turn the water on after several tries. It splashed over the edges of the sink and covered both me and the fiery notebook in a slosh of cold water. Grabbing a tea towel, I swung it back and forth to clear the smoke, opening a window to let the fumes out. The chill from outside blew into the kitchen and the sweet relief of the coldness covered my sweaty skin. After a few more minutes of agony, the alarm finally shut down, leaving me with only Theo's screaming for company.

That and the now sloppy, drowned notebook in the sink.

My heart raced in my chest and my clothes clung to

me in a wet mess, but I didn't care. I was standing in the midst of a disaster and yet all I could do was laugh maniacally as relief crushed down upon me.

Fire be damned—I knew who Henry was following.

Determination settled in the base of my stomach, and I started for the truck, ready to march into an interrogation. My fairy senses tingled under my skin, telling me that I was on the right track. Either that or I was a nervous mess. Fairy senses weren't exactly reliable.

No matter, I had a lead to follow, and I sure wasn't going to sit around making toast for a cat feigning illness. Finn's warning after my trip into the city flashed before me.

I really shouldn't be going alone.

Except Finn was off dealing with the hearing and the police, and I certainly didn't want to tear him away from an important task to gallivant into a possible dead end. For all I knew, Henry had been a deranged man with even more deranged notebooks. Still, I should bring someone along, even if it was only to keep me company on the drive.

I picked up my purse, digging out my cellphone from the bottomless pit and dialed a saved number. The line rang a few times before an aggravated voice sounded on the other end.

"Hello?"

I smiled. "Hey, Rosemary. Lyra here. Any chance you need a break from your mother right about now?"

I didn't need to wait long for her to answer. There were two things that I could count on the funeral home owner for: good conversation and a desperation to get out of the house. Despite Rosemary being inconvenienced, Mrs. Singh's visit was a real light at the end of my tunnel.

Chapter Twenty-One

I stood outside Eloise Penrose's rental house for the second time in as many weeks, staring at the weathered front door as if it might swing open on its own to invite me in. My heart rattled at an unsteady gait, each beat uneven and too loud in my ears, while my toes curled inside my socks like Theo on the couch after a long day. I rocked back and forth on the heels of my boots; the motion doing little to shake the restless energy creeping up my spine.

Beside me, Rosemary mirrored my unease, though in her case, the effect was less subtle. Her entire body vibrated with nervous tension, the tremors running from her fingertips down to the soles of her shoes, as if she might launch herself into the sky at any moment. I couldn't blame her—it was highly possible that we were about to walk into a terrible situation.

The discovery in Henry's hidden notebook weighed heavily on my mind. The historian was tailing his own niece. Why? I groaned. Because he didn't trust her, that's why. And I certainly didn't either. I knew there was something off about Eloise the first time I met her, my suspicions only solidified by the several times she avoided a second meeting with me. The girl was hiding something.

Could that something be murder?

My phone vibrated in my purse, and I took it out, missing a call from Mortimer by a second. I listened to the voicemail, but it was nothing more than a garbled mess of syllables. Putting the phone away, I turned to Rosemary. "Mortimer called."

"What did he want?"

I shrugged. "No clue. The reception was bad, so I couldn't understand a word."

"He really needs to get better service set up in that cottage. I can never get a hold of him when I need to," Rosemary said. She glanced at the house. "This place is creepy."

I followed her gaze, nodding.

The house remained still, its dark windows offering no hint of movement inside. The crisp air carried the scent of damp leaves and cooling asphalt, but it did nothing to quiet the storm brewing inside me. We were here for a reason, though neither Rosemary nor I seemed eager to take the first step.

"Do you think Eloise is home?" Rosemary asked.

I stretched my neck to see inside the eerie house. "It's not looking good."

"Perhaps we should come back another time?"

The offer was enticing enough to make me want to turn around and march back to the truck, but we had already come this far. Not to mention that pesky gnawing feeling at the base of my stomach that told me to knock on the front door. I rolled out the tense muscles in my shoulders and glared at the house. "We're here now. Let's get it over with and go home," I said. "Chances are she's gone, anyway."

We made our way toward the house with dread curling around us in tight ribbons. Every step that took us closer to Eloise made me wish I'd never discovered the notebook in the first place. Actually, it made me wish I never went to the presentation nor gotten involved with Henry's death. Unfortunately, my other option was to take Rhyven and his dooming presence in town more seriously, and I dreaded that more than being here right now. Besides, finding out who hurt Henry was the right thing to do and Fairy damn me if I wasn't stuck on always doing what was decent.

Thanks for that annoying trait, mom.

We trekked along the disheveled front walkway, wet dead leaves sticking to the soles of our shoes. I cringed at the squishiness beneath me and kept my knees locked to avoid slipping around.

The door grew in size before us. I winced, giving Rosemary a quick apologetic glance before raising my knuckles to the worn-out wood. My knuckles throbbed as I tapped them against the door. Once. Twice. Three times.

After the fourth attempt, I was about to leave when the creaking of the door opening made me pause. A sliver of light streamed out from inside, illuminating a panic-stricken Eloise in a golden glow. The curls of her hair were limned in the light, and it made shadows drop onto her face and under her eyes, making her look all the more somber. Her cheeks were hollow and there were stains on her clothes, telling me it had been some time since she changed them.

I tipped my head to the side, confused. "Hi, Eloise. Is this a bad time?"

"Yes," Henry's niece replied curtly.

Her gaze darted around the front yard and there was a bead of sweat on her forehead that disappeared into the hairs of her eyebrows. Though her figure blocked most of the doorway, I saw several suitcases sitting near the door and a few more boxes down the hallway. My brow creased.

"Are you going away?" I asked, pointing at the luggage.

Eloise blanched. "Leaving, actually. I'm moving out. No point staying around here with my uncle gone."

I side-eyed Rosemary, who shook her head.

"What about the funeral?" I asked.

"I'll be there," Eloise said. "Now, if you don't mind, I must finish packing."

She checked the street again, the motion quick but not lost on me. Something was going on with Henry's niece. I couldn't put my finger on it, but if I had to guess, I'd say she was scared. I glanced over my shoulder.

Of what?

Not giving up, I slid my hand into my purse and pulled out the notebook. As soon as Eloise's eyes landed on the old leather, the color drained from her face. Her jaw set and she swallowed several times as though she hadn't drunk water in hours.

Eloise folded her arms over her chest. "What do you have there?"

"Henry's notebook," I said nonchalantly. "Were you aware that he kept one?"

"I did. But that's not the one he used for work," she replied. "Where did you get it?"

She reached for the book, but I yanked it back right as her fingers brushed the cover. "Did you know your uncle left his work notebook for me?" When Eloise shook her head, her expression that of obvious shock, I added, "And I found this one from something he wrote. I believe he wanted me to find it. Care to guess what's inside?"

I had to admit, my bravery was false, and I was quaking in my boots accosting the girl so brashly, but Eloise didn't appear to notice. In fact, even Rosemary was baffled by my new personality trait—her mouth gaping as she stared at me. It's possible I went a tad overboard because neither woman spoke. For a while.

I rolled my eyes, dangling the notebook between Eloise and me.

"Your uncle was following you," I said sternly. "Did you know that?"

"W-what?" Eloise stuttered.

I flipped open the book. The pages were damp and stained, but the writing I had uncovered was still legible and that was all I needed. Pushing the notebook closer to Eloise, I said, "He was tracking your every move as far back as last year. Now why would he do that? You were his niece, his only heir. Why the lack of trust?"

A flash of panic on Eloise's face made her features twist up, but it was gone instantly. She took the notebook from me, this time without me putting up a fight, and read over the entries noted inside. Her eyes narrowed and widened over and over as she rolled her gaze over the blurry words. It took her a few minutes to get through all the entries. She closed the notebook, then opened it again, bringing out her phone to rest on top of one page. For a second, I thought she was going to take a photo of the entries. Eloise did no such thing. She opened the calendar on her phone and scrolled through it, double checking the entries with the appointments she had on her phone.

She scoffed.

"You're wrong," Eloise said.

I bristled. "What do you mean? Your name is right there."

"It's not me Henry was following." She showed me her calendar as though it would explain any of the nonsense she was spewing. "The dates listed here are all the same ones that I had dates with Duncan on. It was him my uncle followed. I had no idea he knew ..."

Voice trailing off into nothing, she stared blankly at the street, her attention wavering only when a car back-fired somewhere in the distance. Eloise jumped, her hand clutching her heart. The notebook fell from her grip, her phone following it down. They crashed to the ground. I winced as the spiderwebs of broken glass spread on the cellphone's screen.

"Shoot!" Eloise said, dropping to pick up the shattered phone. She turned it on, breathing out in relief when it still worked, and shoved it back in her pocket. "Listen, I need to leave. Now."

I looked at Rosemary, then back at Eloise. "What did you mean by thinking Henry didn't know? Didn't know what?"

"Look, I don't have much time. My flight leaves in a few hours, and I still have packing to do."

"Please, Eloise," I begged. "If there is something you know that might help me figure out what happened to Henry, tell me. You know it wasn't an accident; I can see it on your face."

She bit her lip. "No, it wasn't."

"Then tell me what's happened. I can help."

Eloise shrugged, her posture drooping like a ragdoll. "I doubt you'll be able to do anything," she said. "The mess I'm in ... no one can help me now."

"Let me try," I said. I nudged Rosemary. "We're pretty good at this sort of thing. I promise."

"It started when Henry died, but I knew something was wrong long before that," she said.

"What happened?" Rosemary asked, a warm smile on her face.

Eloise sniffled. "The threats. Someone started threatening me to get me to tell them everything I knew about the ship and that stupid treasure. At first it was only text messages. I thought it was a prank. But then I started getting letters in the mail. Here in the rental. And last week someone was in the house. The place was torn apart; it took me forever to clean it up."

"That's awful! Have you gone to the police?"

"To say what?" Eloise said. "I know who's doing it and he won't stop until he gets what he wants. He is not someone I want to mess with. I'm better off running."

I glanced at the notebook on the floor at her feet. "Duncan. You think Duncan is threatening you? I thought you two were a couple."

"We are. Were." Eloise rubbed her eyes with the heel of her palms. "Don't get me wrong, he didn't force me to date him. I loved him. But there were signs. There always are, aren't there? Duncan never cared about restoring lost history or any of the things my uncle and me value. All he wanted was to make more money. It was never enough."

She breathed out slowly, took another deep breath, and let that one go as well. "I saw one of his paychecks recently and it was an insanely large sum," she said. "At first, I thought it was from Daphne, but why would Daphne be paying so much money? Besides, the logo didn't look like her company's."

"What do you think the money was for?" I asked.

"Isn't it obvious?" Eloise said. "To get closer to me and my uncle. To find out about the ship."

I rubbed my chin. "What did the logo look like?"

"I barely recall now. A weird design. Two buckets I think, but I'm not sure." She checked her watch. "But I have to go. Duncan could be here at any moment and if he sees you two, there's no knowing what he'll do. I've been keeping him busy by giving him random tasks to do while he was in town, pretending he was helping me with the funeral."

"That's why he showed up at my door," I mumbled.

Eloise's lips pressed into a thin red line. "Sorry about that. I needed him gone so I could book my flight and plan my escape."

She checked her watch once more, signaling that we needed to give the woman her space. I took a step back. Pulling out my business card, I handed it to Eloise, making sure she took it before saying, "If you feel like you're in danger, call me. Day or night."

"Thank you," Eloise said, pocketing the card. "Truly. I hope you can find a way to figure out what happened to Henry. Promise me that if Duncan is involved, you'll let me know. I wish I could help with more, but my uncle did not share the details of his work with me. He said it was safer that way." She blinked rapidly. "I'm starting to see that he was right. That ship is going to get both of us killed."

"Not if I can help it," I promised.

We left Eloise to her packing. As we drove off, I asked Rosemary to give the police station a call to ask someone to drive by in the next hour. Just in case. My fingers gripped the wheel, and the backs of my legs sweated in my jeans. The leather of the seat was suddenly suffocating. Mind racing, I repeated Eloise's description of the logo in my head. Two buckets. Two buckets. Two—

I veered the truck off the road and onto the shoulder. Gravel spun from under the wheels and the screech made Rosemary gasp. I looked at her, my mouth wide open.

They weren't buckets. They were scales.

I'd seen the image of the logo before, and it was right before Henry was killed. I knew who paid off Duncan. And possibly who killed our town's historian ...

Chapter Twenty-Two

I left Rosemary at the secret library with the promise of returning with the rest of the team. Finn had texted while we were on the road to let me know he was on his way and Ellie was about to join after she wrapped up with a body preparation. But Mortimer was nowhere to be found. I knew the ancient mortician often turned his phone off, so it was easier to swing by his place to pick him up than impatiently wait by the phone. My nerves were at an all time high as it was.

I couldn't believe that the person responsible for paying off Duncan was right under our noses. And we even met him briefly!

My thoughts raced back to the day of the presentation and the strange historian we spoke to before Henry came on stage. Oliver Hodge. The man with the dapper outfit and the bronze pin of the scales on his lapel. The one that mentioned knowing Henry professionally.

It bothered me that I hadn't considered him as a suspect prior to this. In my defense, I hadn't thought of Oliver since that meeting, and at the time, I had no reason to link him to Henry's death. But now that I knew he had been paying Duncan for information on Henry and the ship, I couldn't think of anything else. Every conversation, every clue I had gathered over the last few weeks, took on a new shape in my mind.

I thought back to my meeting with Daphne; the moment coming into sharp, almost painful clarity. She had mentioned another historian—a man who had been asking questions, sniffing around the same leads. At the time, I had dismissed it as coincidence, assuming it was only another researcher chasing a curiosity. But now, the pieces clicked into place.

Oliver. It had to be him.

There weren't many historians with connections to Radcliffe and Henry Barlow, and even fewer with a vested interest in the sunken ship. He fit the profile too perfectly. He had been circling this mystery, digging for information just like I had, but with a motive I had been too blind to see. Was it simply professional interest? A need to uncover the ship's secrets before anyone else? Or was it something more selfish and monetary?

My stomach tightened. If Oliver had been looking into Henry's past—paying for scraps of information, working in the shadows—what exactly had he been hoping to find? And more importantly, how far would he go to keep it hidden?

I gritted my teeth, turning the truck down the gravel winding road between tall, towering pines. Mortimer lived on the other side of town in a remote cabin tucked deep inside the Orchard Hollow woods. It was a picturesque location and reminded me a lot of Fairy, down to the fact that it was nearly impossible to get to. For all its privacy, Mortimer's cabin was nestled so deep in the woods that it didn't show up on my GPS. I only knew how to get here based on Rosemary's very detailed directions.

On either side of me, trees rose high in the sky, obscuring the sun and painting the path ahead a dark shade of gloom. The silence in the woods was unnerving with only the occasional flap of wings overhead as birds took off from branches. There was a snap of twigs that echoed somewhere in the distance. My stomach dropped.

I rolled up the windows to keep the sounds of nature out and continued to crawl on at a snail's pace. The truck's wheels spun on the unfinished road and stones jumped out on all sides, ricocheting off tree trunks like bullets.

Mortimer was a real champ for making the drive out here daily.

The scenery of the forest unfolded beyond the windshield. Small ponds peeked out from overgrown bushes and several clearings broke the wall of trees every once in a while. It truly was magical.

I swerved left and onto another path, this one narrower and ultimately darker. The deeper I drove, the more the forest closed in around me. The trees stood taller here, their gnarled branches intertwining over-head, blocking out what little light tried to seep through. Shadows stretched long across the narrow road—if you could call it that—flickering in my headlights like tiny ghosts. The air felt heavier. More still. As if the world outside had stopped breathing. Although maybe that was just me.

I kept my hands tight on the wheel, easing forward at a careful pace. The gravel gave way to packed dirt, and the ruts in the road shook the truck, making the dashboard rattle. I could see the clearing just ahead and a small cottage between the trees.

The steeply pitched roof was blanketed in moss that seemed wet from the moist surroundings. A squat chimney jutted from one side. Without a ribbon of smoke curling toward the sky, it was hard to tell if it worked and I hoped for Mortimer's sake it did since the woods were particularly cold today. The small-paned windows of the cottage were empty black squares, no lights pouring out from within.

Was Mortimer not home? I pulled in closer and narrowed my eyes as his home came into clearer view.

The cottage's front porch was a simple wooden platform that sagged slightly in one corner where the wood had started to come apart, bordered with a railing just sturdy enough to lean against. A set of wind chimes hung beside the door, their silver tubes swaying to a sweet little melody that made no rhythmic sense. A cluster of potted plants sat on the steps and, much like my roses, they were in full bloom. Mortimer may not have been a fairy, but he sure had a green thumb.

Not far from me, an owl hooted, the sound sharp and sudden in the hush of the woods. I pressed on the gas and accelerated the truck into the driveway, relieved when I spotted Mortimer's car parked around the side of the house.

But something was wrong.

The house was dark. As were the surroundings with the trees so dense in this part of the woods. There wasn't a porch light on and no sign of movement inside. I got out of the truck, my breath shaky.

"Mortimer?" I yelled out.

I was answered only by more dreadful silence. Stomping through an overgrown grassy area, I crept to the front door. My heart beat loudly between my ears as my gaze fell on the small open crevice of the door.

Mortimer was meticulous—he never would have left without securing everything, without locking up tight, especially in a place this remote. But now, the front door stood slightly open, just enough to let someone slip in.

My pulse jumped. Somehow, the thought of stepping into the cottage sent a shiver down my spine and the pep in my step slowed to nonexistence.

A gust of wind stirred the branches of the trees at my back, rustling the leaves to hurry me along. I swallowed hard.

Something about the house felt wrong.

I reached for the door handle, took a breath, and walked in.

"Mortim—"

A hard, blunt object crashed into the back of my head before I could finish the word. It fell away from my lips, drifting into the emptiness of the cottage. My vision swam and black dots swarmed in, making me lose my balance. I shot a hand out for leverage, but depth perception was no longer my friend and I stutter-stepped to the side, my shoulder colliding with a large wardrobe. My legs were liquid—too weak to hold up the weight of my body.

Something wet dripped down my neck and I shivered, pressing my palm to the rear of my head. It came away sticky and smelling of iron.

I worked to blink away the dots and focus my eyes, but everything inside the cottage swam before me. Knees hitting the ground first, I went down like a rock.

"M ... M ..."

There was no air in my lungs. Lips dry, I struggled to get up again, but it was too hard, and the floor was so close and welcoming. I laid my head down, the cold hardwood pressing to my cheek. Suddenly, my legs were yanked by someone strong, and I was dragged from the front door and into the abyss of the house. Splinters tore at my skin as my arms dragged over the floor.

The person moving me stopped, letting my legs crash down with a loud, unforgiving thud. I wanted to groan, but even that was too much effort.

In the distance, I thought I heard a familiar voice telling me to stay awake, but it was muffled by all the noise in my head. It sounded like a fan was on full blast up here. A final breath expelled from my tired lungs right before the voice finally made sense.

"Stay with me, Lyra!" Mortimer screamed.

I could not oblige.

My lids drooped, and I closed my eyes, letting sleep take me away.

Chapter Twenty-Three

A dull, throbbing ache anchored me to the ground before I had a chance to even open my eyes. My head felt heavy, stuffed with cotton and lead, like my brain was trying to swim through syrup. My limbs felt as though I had gotten caught in fairy vines. I forced a breath, slow and shallow, and a metallic taste of blood coated my tongue.

My fingers twitched against something rough. Carpet? No—hardwood. The last few minutes slowly came back to me as panic set in. I recalled arriving at Mortimer's cottage. I remembered the open door. Then ...

Nothing.

I tried to move, but a fresh wave of pain crashed over me, radiating from the back of my skull. I groaned and forced my eyes open. The world tilted. Shadows blurred and shifted. My stomach lurched.

How in the fairy wings did I continue to get knocked out in these wild scenarios? If I knew having friends would come with this many concussions, I may have reconsidered joining the Wardens.

I blinked away the blurriness from my vision.

What happened?

The realization sent a fresh spike of fear through my chest. My pulse stuttered, then pounded, too fast, too loud. I pushed up on trembling arms, ignoring the fire in my muscles, the way my head spun like I was still falling.

Someone was in Mortimer's house when I arrived, and they hurt me enough to knock me out. But that's not the only thing my brain clutched onto. Mortimer was here. I heard him calling for me before I lost consciousness.

I looked around the dimly lit cottage and tried to figure out which part of the house I was in. Shelves towering to the ceiling spread out before me, covering every available wall. On them, plants cascaded from pots and filled the shelves with shades of green and yellow and brown. The overwhelming amount of oxygen in the room made my head spin harder, and I fought against it to sit upright. The air was muggy and thick, and I instantly knew where I was.

Mortimer has a greenhouse.

"Lyra? Oh, thank goodness you're awake."

I turned my head to the right, the motion rattling through my brain like a piñata. Tucked into the greenhouse corner, Mortimer watched me with careful eyes, his arms behind his back. Tied, I wagered.

My lips cracked into a soft smile. "Oliver is here, isn't he?"

"I'm afraid so," Mortimer said.

"Why did he come here?" I asked. Giving it a bit of thought, I stopped myself from continuing. "You figured it out before I did."

Mortimer shrugged. "Guilty. I tracked Duncan's bank deposits thanks to a friend at his bank in the city. They led me to the professor." He rearranged himself, the movement clearly painful as he winced visibly from the effort. "I wanted to check it out before raising alarm bells with you all, so I called Oliver and pretended to want to discuss Henry's presentation; went as far as to invite him over. He must have caught on because the next thing I knew, I was being held at gunpoint in my own living room."

"Safe to assume we were both right to suspect him," I said dimly. "I wish we weren't. Do you think he killed Henry to get to the treasure?"

"It's more complicated than that, I fear," Mortimer answered.

I arched a brow at him. "Because the treasure was fake. Henry was lying about the entire thing. He never found a thing."

There was a prolonged silence. Mortimer watched me carefully, his eyes rounding as he did. His lips parted, a sigh following the exhale.

"I'm sorry your friend wasn't who you thought he was," he finally said. "But you should know, I discovered something else when I was investigating Oliver Hodge."

"What's that?"

"Henry wasn't working on the scam alone."

I gulped, my lungs constricting. "You don't mean ..."

The nod of agreement from Mortimer had me twisted up inside. Every notion I had of Henry before came crashing down with a loud bang of cymbals in the background to accommodate the demise of his character. As though it wasn't bad enough that Henry's code of honor was dangerously skewed, but now to find out that he was in cahoots with a man like Oliver, someone willing to kill for ... Well, I wasn't sure what, actually. Still, it was enough to make me think that the Henry I knew was nothing more than a lie. A made-up personality created to impress when the real man underneath the facade was a scam artist at best.

Bile swirled inside my stomach.

"But why?" I asked. "Why bother going to all this

trouble to falsify a treasure most people had given up on anyhow?"

Mortimer's shoulders hiked up to his ears, then dropped again. "I didn't have the chance to find out on account of being nearly killed. Then you showed up."

The greenhouse door creaked open, and a gust of wind blew inside. The plants rustled and recoiled. I followed suit. A wide frame filled the doorway—Oliver Hodge. The glint of bronze on his jacket made my teeth grind, and I flicked my gaze to the pretentious college pin on his jacket.

I set my jaw.

"You're not going to get away with this, Oliver," I said. "This isn't the same as faking a projector accident. You're holding two people hostage."

The professor narrowed his eyes at my crouching form. "Don't worry, Miss Moore. I have a plan."

"I called the police."

Oliver reached into his jacket pocket and pulled out a familiar cellphone. He held it out, showing me my phone like I didn't already know who it belonged to.

The professor sneered. "No, you didn't. It would have been smart to do so, by the way." He reached into his jacket again, this time pulling out the gun Mortimer mentioned before. "In case you get any bright ideas."

Little did he know, I already wasted all my bright

ideas before I got here. I swallowed the lump in my throat.

"What are you going to do with us?" I asked. "People will be looking for us. And surely the police will get involved. Are you really willing to risk everything for a fake treasure?"

A loud, mocking cackle burst from Oliver's lips. He looked down at me from the doorway, his sneer growing in size. From this vantage point, he looked very much the part of the villain role he chose to fill. "You think this is about what? Fame?" he asked incredulously. "You're no better than Henry. That was all he cared about, too. *People will have to believe us now, Oliver. They will have to listen, Oliver. We can get the funding we need to start a proper research team, Oliver,*" the professor mocked. "He was insufferable."

"And you killed him for it?"

Oliver's features darkened into something I couldn't discern. He wiped his brow with the back of his hand, the metal of the gun dazzling when the light from the single bulb in the greenhouse hit it. "I killed him because he wouldn't listen to reason," he said. "Henry grew a conscience in his older age—probably to appease that niece of his. He wanted to come clean about what we were planning, to thwart our entire plan. We had everything figured out. Falsify the evidence about the

Hollow Siren and use it to secure grants for discovery missions. To secure our future."

"But you wouldn't have found anything," I said. "The ship was already discovered. Nothing was aboard."

"It would be easy enough to dispose of that bit of information," Oliver rebutted. "We already had several grants approved! Money that we needed. That *I* needed. But no, Henry had to spoil it all."

I shook my head, disbelief coating the inside of my mouth in an acidic flavor. "You killed your friend for money?"

"Henry was no friend of mine," Oliver sniped. "Not after he betrayed me. Do you think they would simply pat us on the hand and tell us to go on our merry way once the jig was up? Of course not! We committed fraud! I'd be fired from the college. Not to mention the lawsuits that would pile up. Historians don't make millions, you know. I'd be ruined."

Suddenly, the checks to Duncan made a lot more sense. I grunted, sitting up taller and straighter. "You paid Duncan to sabotage the projector, didn't you?"

"That buffoon?" Oliver huffed out. "Heavens no. The wannabe treasure hunter found out that Henry was lying about the ship. I had to pay him off to get him off our backs."

"With the grant money," Mortimer cut in.

Oliver nodded. "Now you see my dilemma. If the truth came out, I'd have to give all that money back. Money I no longer had to give."

"But what about—"

The barrel of the gun pointed at my chest. "I think that's enough chit chat for the time being," Oliver said. "I'm afraid you know too much as it is."

His finger idled on the trigger and for a moment, I thought he might change his mind. It wasn't until Oliver's shoulders squared and his jaw tightened that I realized my fate was sealed. I glanced at Mortimer. Both our fates. My legs tightened, and I shifted around so I could stand up quickly. I had no chance of outrunning the bullet, but maybe if I acted fast enough, I could tackle the professor and buy Mortimer some time to escape. It was the only way one of us would get out of this alive.

I locked gazes with Mortimer and pressed my lips together into a sad smile.

Oliver's finger squeezed.

Leaping forward, I threw myself at the man. My body sliced through the air and kept flying. Past the space Oliver stood at just a moment before and through the doorway. My chest hit the ground first, a sharp pain radiating through my lungs and into my upper back. I groaned, twisting around, and looked in through the still open doorway.

My jaw hit the ground.

Lying on the floor of the greenhouse was Oliver. There was a shattered pot next to his head and dark red liquid oozed from the fresh wound in his matted hair. His arms splayed on either side of him and his chest rose up and down so slowly I almost didn't see it move. Shadows swirled over Oliver's limp body and filled the greenhouse until it was nearly entirely pitch black. Towering over the professor was another figure. A tall, dark, and horrifyingly familiar one.

I gasped. "Rhyven."

The Prince of the Shadow Court flicked his wrists and the shadows emanating from his being recoiled back into his body. He rolled out his shoulders, his eyebrows slanting. Eyes the color of sapphires pinned me in place, and his square jaw set as he inspected my crumpled form beneath him.

"You live an adventurous life," he said, his voice smooth as butter. "I'll give you that."

The prince stalked toward me like a predator to prey. I scrambled backward, my butt scraping against the dirt. When he reached me, Rhyven did something I didn't expect. He didn't end my life right there and then. He didn't yank me by my hair and drag my sorry behind back to Fairy. He didn't even scold me.

Instead, the prince held out his hand and said, "You don't have to be afraid."

Disbelief flooded my system.

"Wait, what?" I asked, shaking. "Aren't you here to punish me for escaping?"

Rhyven's eyes flashed, and his nose flared. "I should have found a way to come to you sooner." He rubbed his temples. "I'm not going to hurt you, Lyra. Quite the opposite. I have come to this strange realm to prove to you that you need not be afraid. I want you to come back, Summer Princess, but only on your terms."

"And what terms would those be?"

"That you trust me enough to accept my proposal," Rhyven said. "Your hand in marriage should be by choice. I know that now and I want you to choose me as I have chosen you."

Seriously, what now?

I glared at the prince without a word. Then a memory made all the anger I felt rush to the surface, and I jumped up to stand, cocking my hip to the side and crossing my arms over my chest. "What about my cat?"

"The changeling?" Rhyven asked. "What about him?"

"You've been threatening him since you got here! And you poisoned him."

Rhyven chuckled, the muscles in his wide chest rippling. "I didn't threaten the changeling."

"You left a note!"

"I left a warning," Rhyven corrected. "That cat gets into a lot of things on your property when you aren't home. Things like the geraniums you keep in your backyard."

I bit down on my tongue. Why would Theo be messing about with the garden?

As if guessing my thoughts, Rhyven said, "He's been burying things there. Things he steals from you when you're not home."

My body stilled. The missing watch, the earrings, the gold pen. It all made sense now. Theo was the one taking my things. That dreadful changeling and his obsession with shiny objects! My heart raced as another realization hit me.

"I use eggshells in the soil for the geraniums," I whispered.

"Correct," Rhyven said. "And changelings are dreadfully allergic to them."

I slapped my head. "Theo poisoned himself. The little fool. What about my roses?"

"What about them?"

A growl reverberated deep inside my chest. "You turned them purple. Why?"

Rhyven's featured contorted, and he cocked his head to the side, his brows knitting together.

"That wasn't you, was it?" I asked.

He shook his head. "You see? You have nothing to fear."

I'd be the judge of that. If it wasn't Rhyven that

messed up my flowers, then ... Wonderful. Another manifestation of my bizarre fae powers making an ugly appearance. I didn't even know what this one may have meant. Perhaps my mood affected them? I'd have to do some research at another date when I wasn't being glared at by the Prince of the Shadow Court.

The prince extended his hand again, but I slapped it away, brushing past him. I walked a few more steps to put some distance between us before turning to look at him over my shoulder. "If you truly want me to trust you," I said. "You will leave now. I have enough explaining to do as it is. Your shadow display will need a story."

With a nod, Rhyven backed away, his arms up in surrender.

"I'll wait for you, Lyra," he said. "For as long as it takes."

Then a whirl of darkness spread around him, and he vanished like he was never there. I sucked in a sharp breath, slouching as I made my way back inside the greenhouse. Rhyven may have saved my life today, but it didn't mean he didn't bring more trouble to my doorstep. My attention caught on Mortimer's bulging eyes and his questioning expression.

For starters, I had to come up with an excuse for what the mortician just witnessed and it had better be good enough to keep me out of the mental institution.

Chapter Twenty-Four

If you thought that convincing someone they didn't just witness an out-of-this-world act of magic through the sheer force of your theatrical performance would be tough, you'd be absolutely correct. In fact, I'd rank it somewhere between explaining taxes to a werewolf and trying to politely decline a deal from a fae without ending up in a lifelong magical contract.

Mortimer, bless his stubborn human heart, wasn't making it easy. He kept insisting—*insisting*—that there had been another man in the room, a shadowy figure who had appeared at the perfect moment, intervened, and then promptly vanished like a well-timed magician's assistant. And of course, he just *had* to bring it up over and over again while I was trying to focus on making sure Oliver didn't wake up and try something stupid, like escaping or trying to kill us again.

I did my best to keep my expression neutral, even though I could feel my heart still rattling against my ribs from the whole debacle. "Mortimer," I said in my calmest, most patient tone, the kind you use on someone who is determined to argue that pineapple belongs on pizza. "We were both under a lot of stress. That sort of thing can play tricks on the mind. Your brain filled in the gaps, that's all. It's basic psychology."

To his credit, he didn't outright scoff, but the squint he leveled at me could have cut glass. "Basic psychology?"

"Yes," I said, putting a hand over my heart in what I hoped was a convincing show of solidarity. "Stress. Adrenaline. Darkness. Your brain just ... connected some dots in a strange way."

He crossed his arms. "My brain connected some dots in a strange way."

"That's what I said."

He looked unconvinced. Extremely unconvinced. But thankfully, I didn't have to keep spinning my web of plausible deniability much longer, because that was right about when the police showed up, sirens wailing, throwing a whole new level of chaos into the mix.

The good news? Mortimer was quickly swept up in the

madness of explaining why Oliver had a gun, why I had tackled him, and what in Fairy's name had led to this mess in the first place. Between the notebooks Henry left for me, the secret house on Coroner Street, and Oliver's own admittance while threatening us, the police had an easy case on their hands. Sure, there would still be a trial, but I had the inkling it would not go well for Oliver Hodge. Especially if they got Eloise and Duncan to testify against him.

But no fairy tale is complete without an obstacle. Which brought me to the bad news. I still had at least two different crises waiting in the wings, including—but not limited to—the *actual* man of shadow who saved us, and the fact that my changeling cat had apparently been moonlighting as a small-time criminal for who knows how long.

One problem at a time, I reminded myself.

Mortimer had, for now, at least temporarily set aside his questions about our mysterious helper, and I wasn't about to remind him. That was future me's disaster to deal with.

Present me, however, had much more pressing issues.

For instance, why my cat was currently watching me from the morgue doorway with an expression so smug it should have been illegal, a shiny new bracelet sitting between his front paws like a prize?

I sighed, rubbing my temples. "Where did you get that?"

Changeling cats. I swear, they're worse than toddlers.

"Nowhere," the cat said.

I rolled my eyes. "Theo, come on! You need to stop this nonsense. You literally almost died because you can't keep your grubby paws off shiny things."

"I can't help it," Theo drawled. "It's in my DNA. Now, if you'll excuse me, I need to make a deposit."

He trotted away with my bracelet clutched in his feline teeth like a vise. I didn't need to follow the cat to know where he went. Ever since Rhyven told me that Theo had been burying his stolen goods in the backyard, I proposed an alternate solution. It seemed it did not take much convincing to get the cat to change out his hiding spot. Granted, I had to give up my attic for him to use, but it was worth it—I didn't know what I would do if I lost the thieving changeling.

In the end, we were both pleased. Theo got to keep stashing his trinkets to appease his changeling needs, and I got to keep the cat healthy and breathing. Win-win!

I did sorely miss some of my jewelry, though.

A loud knock at the front door reverberated through the manor, making my skin break out in goosebumps. I put down the scalpel and took off the medical gloves, tossing the balled-up plastic into a garbage bin. After zipping up the body bag, I rolled dear old Mr. Mandrok back into a freezer unit, rolled down my sleeves, and walked up the stairs.

My footsteps echoed through the house. I felt light, feathery even, after finally putting the business of Henry's death to bed. Or six feet under in this case, as the funeral was yesterday, and the historian could finally be put to rest. The service was perfection and exactly as Henry envisioned it. And it was lovely to see Eloise again.

Despite Duncan no longer being a threat, Eloise arrived alone, her black coat wrapped tightly around her as if shielding herself from more than just the chill. She moved quietly when she came into the service, shoulders squared, chin high, her eyes unreadable as they flicked over the assembled mourners before settling on the casket. It took me most of the service to work up the nerve to speak to her, but when I did, I was glad for it. After the funeral finished, we ended up in my kitchen chatting for a while over a warm cup of tea. Henry's niece was lovely to speak with, and quite the chatterbox when she wasn't afraid for her life. When I asked her why Duncan didn't make it to the service, she couldn't stop herself from talking.

According to her, even if the treasure hunter hadn't stooped to the violence she'd once feared, his willingness to take bribes and withhold the truth had been enough to sever their relationship beyond repair. Betrayal, even in its lesser forms, was still betrayal. She might not have known about Duncan's affair, but at this point, it hardly mattered. The damage was done, the trust nonexistent between them. And so, I kept my mouth shut.

Not that I needed to. There wasn't a chance in Fairy Eloise would ever take the slimeball back. I could see it in the set of her jaw, in the way her fingers curled into fists at her sides when she mentioned his name. She was as unyielding as her uncle had been—the one admirable trait of Henry's to pass on. If nothing else, at least she had his spine.

Lucky for everyone, Eloise didn't inherit Henry's scamming ways. She even planned to make things right after Henry's disaster and devote her time to finding the real history of the Hollow Siren and bringing it to light. Starting with putting the rumors of the treasure to bed once and for all.

It was a nice gesture considering the mess her uncle had started.

I unlocked the front door and slid the chain off the hook, stepping back to allow for the door to open. The porch flowers were back in full bloom and the smell of roses wafted into the manor, making my senses jump to attention. My fingers twitched with the need to touch the flowers. I fought against it, focusing on the man standing on the porch.

Finn was an exceptional type of handsome today with his hair tousled and his jaw dusted in a five o'clock shadow. The newsboy cap he often wore sat low on his brow and as he looked at me through thick lashes, my brain forgot how to work. I mumbled syllables that didn't make it to full words under my breath, my palms slick with sweat.

"Hey Lyra," the morgue director said.

I opened my mouth for a second attempt at normalcy and failed again.

After a few deep breaths, I finally managed to croak out a meager, "Hello."

"I wanted to stop by to see how you're holding up," Finn said, removing his cap. The leather of his jacket strained against his biceps. My cheeks burned. "After what happened, I mean."

"Oh. I'm doing all right. Have you talked to Mortimer?"

I had to admit that my motives for asking were two-fold. Sure, I wanted to know how the mortician was holding up, but I could have just as easily asked him myself. The real reason was because I wished to see what he may have said to Finn about a certain dark prince and his creepy shadow magic.

When Finn smiled, I let the bundle of nerves in my throat loosen.

"He's back to his usual self," Finn said. "Which is to say frustrating and overly detail oriented."

I chuckled. "That's good to hear. It was quite the scene at his house."

"He's lucky you were there. That was real quick thinking to tackle Oliver. Weren't you afraid he'd shoot?"

"Definitely," I admitted. "But I figured Mortimer had a shot to escape if I moved quickly enough. It was worth the gamble."

Finn's eyes sparkled. "You are an extraordinary woman, Lyra Moore," he said. "One I would still very much like to take out to dinner. If you're up for it, that is."

My eyes flicked around the porch, the hairs on my neck standing straight up. I glanced over my shoulder into the depths of the manor. The door to the morgue stood ajar, beckoning me to hours of work. I had a lot to catch up on today and this week in general. When I agreed to join the Grim Wardens, I hadn't realized how much of my time chasing leads and solving crimes would take. These days my schedule was nearly overtaken with Warden business, and I didn't want it to take over my life. As fun as working with the undertakers was, it didn't exactly pay the bills around here.

The outside air cooled my overheated face. I blanched, looking up at Finn.

"I kind of have a lot to get through here today," I said.

Finn shot his hands up in surrender. "I didn't mean right this second," he said warmly. "But sooner rather than later. How about Friday night? We can end our busy weeks with a nice meal."

"In that case, it's a date!" I announced.

"Great. Let's make sure to follow through this time," Finn teased. He put his cap back on and tipped it my way. "I'll let you get back to work. Can't wait for Friday."

"Oh, I meant to ask, how did things turn out with the court case?"

Finn's teeth flashed. "All settled. Your tip to talk to the sheriff paid off and I'm off the hook." He winked. "Like I said, extraordinary."

Before I had a chance to overthink, to fumble over my words or do something clumsy that would break the perfection of the moment, Finn leaned in. His breath was warm against my skin, a flutter of fairy wings, and then his lips pressed softly to my cheek. The touch was brief, but it sent a shiver through me, stealing the air from my lungs.

And then it was gone. The warmth of his lips faded,

replaced by a chill that made me wish I could pull him back, just for a second longer.

I smiled, my fingers twitching at my side, resisting the urge to reach up and trace the spot where his lips had been. Instead, I lifted my hand in a wave, my gaze following him as he walked down the steps. I could watch that man walk away forever and never tire of it—though, if I had my way, I'd much rather watch him come back.

"You're drooling."

I cringed, turning around to face Theo. "How long have you been sitting there?"

"Long enough to see you ogle the morgue director," he said. "You know, I'm awfully proud of you. Stringing two men along ... I didn't think you had it in you."

I shooed him off of my shoes.

"I'm not stringing anyone around. Rhyven is—" I considered my choice of words "—a complication. But my opinion of the prince had not changed. He can wait around all he wishes; I am not going back to Fairy."

"Settling for the human?" Theo mused. "Interesting."

Annoyance zoomed through my system. What was Theo on about? I wasn't settling for anyone. Finn was a wonderful man, a catch. If I'd be settling, it would be to choose the Shadow Court Prince. I hadn't forgotten his cruel family, nor the way he used to behave as a child.

Whatever pretenses Rhyven was here under, it wasn't to win me back.

Yet he did save me ...

I groaned, frustrated. Inside the confines of my body, my magic stirred and vibrated. I stomped my foot to get it to calm down, but it had the opposite effect. Sparks of rainbow magic shot out from my chest and into the hallway, lighting it up like fireworks. My teeth split apart as the magic swirled in a tornado that sparkled so brightly, I had to shield my eyes. It continued to pick up speed, knocking frames off the wall and vases off the side table. Glass and ceramic shards burst on the floor. I jumped out of the way, grabbing Theo to shield him from the blast.

A few moments passed while my magic continued to wreak havoc on the manor. Then, it evaporated like a summer storm in the tropics. Gone entirely. Well, not entirely.

In the exact spot where my magic-fueled tornado had raged only moments ago, a portal now stood—tall, narrow, and shimmering like the surface of a restless lake. The edges flickered as the light wavered, shifting from the realm I stood in to whatever lay beyond the doorway. Colors bled and reformed, a swirling mirage of two worlds colliding.

I hesitated, then took a cautious step forward and peered inside. A blast of icy air slammed into me, sharp as needles against my skin. My breath hitched as frost bloomed across my cheeks and icicles formed on the tip of my nose. Shaking, I brushed them away, but my fingers were stiff, my skin already numbing from the cold.

Beyond the threshold, an endless winter stretched before me. Mountains, their peaks covered in ice, loomed against a slate-gray sky. Snow blanketed the landscape in a desolate expanse, the vastness of it all making my chest tighten. A storm churned in the distance, wind howling, and for a moment, I swore I could feel it inside the manor.

I stumbled back, putting much-needed distance between myself and whatever frigid nightmare I had just unlocked. My gaze darted to Theo, who cuddled into my chest, his tail flicking in disapproval.

"That's not our home," the cat noted dryly, his golden eyes narrowing.

My heart pounded, my fingers curling into fists as a terrible dread took hold. My eyes doubled in size.

Fairy help me. What did I do this time?

About the Author

A.N. Sage is a bestselling, award-winning author of mystery and fantasy novels. She has spent most of her life waiting to meet a witch, vampire, or at least get haunted by a ghost. In between failed seances and many questionable outfit choices, she has developed a keen eye for the extra-ordinary.

A.N. spends her free time reading and binge-watching television shows in her pajamas. Currently, she resides in Toronto, Canada with her husband who is not a creature of the night and their daughter who just might be.

A.N. Sage is a Scorpio and a massive advocate of leggings for pants.

For more books and updates:

www.ansage.ca

Connect on social media:

Facebook Group:

facebook.com/groups/945090619339423/

Instagram:

instagram.com/a.n.sage/

YouTube:

youtube.com/c/ANSageWrites

www.ingramcontent.com/pod-product-compliance
Lightning Source LLC
Chambersburg PA
CBHW020419110726
47899CB00006B/2053